"Let's take the bastards." He unholstered the M61 Skorpion and unfolded the wire stock. It was clipped and ready to rock. The blond headman of ICE adjusted his vest flaps so the standby clips were easy to reach. He threaded the Skorpion silencer on the barrel.

Dartanian looked over at Larry LaSalle. The ex-cop had a salt-and-pepper beard and mustache left over from his undercover days. He looked like he belonged in a café debating Gurdjieff with a raven haired poetess—not in a dimmed hallway outside a slave lord's card party with a sub in his hands.

The noise from the men inside increased. Someone told a joke. Someone swore. They were having a hell of a time.

"Fire a foot high and wave it," Dartanian said. "Like this." He demonstrated the technique by gently lifting and lowering the Skorpion. Firing at a one-foot level would catch them if they dived to the floor for cover. If not, their legs would get chopped down in a hurry. "Do the second clip waist high." The second volley would take care of anyone who wised up and sought cover a foot off the floor.

"Got it," LaSalle said.

"Then hit it." Dartanian squeezed the trigger. Chunks of wood dropped to the floor. The 7.65mm rounds ate through the thin plasterboard. Dartanian stitched the apartment wall from right to left. The *phyyyt-phyyt* sound of the silenced Skorpion was drowned out by the screams inside.

THE PROTECTOR

Rich Rainey

#1 VENUS UNDERGROUND

PINNACLE BOOKS **NEW YORK**

THE PROTECTOR #1: VENUS UNDERGROUND

Copyright © 1982 by Rich Rainey

An original Pinnacle Books edition, published for the first time anywhere.

First printing, November 1982

ISBN: 0-523-41849-3

Cover illustration by George Wilson

Printed in the United States of America

PINNACLE BOOKS, INC.
1430 Broadway
New York, New York 10018

VENUS UNDERGROUND

Prologue

The tall bearded Jamaican sat across from the only other passenger on the subway car and stared hard, as though he could see right through the man's newspaper. Razor enjoyed waiting for his victims to see him close up. The best part was the look, the last look before he struck.

This was his turf, this mobile jungle clattering and hurtling through the dark caves of the city. He felt at home in the graffiti scarred boxes, especially at night.

"Look at de busynessmon. He all alone. He think Razor no see him behind dat paper. But Razor Mikey see everything." The words came out low and animal-like; the muscled giant in the sleeveless sweatshirt was an animal.

The man behind the DAILY NEWS wore a light blue suit. His blond mustache was clipped square and short. He read the news calmly and smoked a Pall Mall as the raving maniac eyed him.

"I think, man, I had enough of dis playtime."

The man lowered the newspaper just below his eyes.

1

Razor smiled, flicked a long straight razor, and slashed it through the air. He widened his eyes to mock his victim while he waited for the last gasp.

The man in the suit calmly pressed his cigarette into the paper. It browned, blackened, and then whispered into flame. Six-inch spears of fire sprouted into the air.

Razor cocked his head in disbelief before the man threw the burning paper into his face. The Jamaican screamed and slashed wildly at the newspaper, but the flames captured his beard in a wicked burst.

The man stood, cocked his knee, and planted his heel deep into the Jamaican's chest.

Razor grunted as his head snapped forward.

Then, as if he was driving a railroad spike, the man whipped a hammerfist to the back of Razor's neck. There was a quick crack.

The Jamaican bounced back into his seat and slumped forward, dead beneath the falling embers.

The man got off at the next stop.

Now the subway, Razor Mikey's home, was Razor Mikey's coffin. The wake was open to the public.

Alex Dartanian was a businessman, as the Jamaican had guessed, but it was a special kind of business. He was head of Dartanian Security Service. DSS was composed of over one hundred operatives, half of them shuffling back and forth from government assignments to private practice.

The headquarters on Cage Street served as a clearinghouse for hordes of government lettermen. The CIA, NSA, and DEA moved like clandestine monks keeping the flame alive.

Dartanian permitted the agencies to use DSS as a front; they let him use the agencies as a front. Whenever he needed credentials for tricky assignments, they gave them to him. Dartanian controlled a shadowy network of fronts, dummy corporations, and the daily business of DSS.

It was an agency capable of forming or tearing apart a government. Dartanian could assemble a hit team or make certain that Mr. and Mrs. Jones had a safe night on the town. It was spy heaven and he was St. Peter standing at the gates with a M61 Skorpion submachine gun strapped to his wings.

The public knew him as the Protector, the best in the business. A few core members of DSS knew him as something more. Dartanian was the leader of ICE, the ultimate ghost group.

ICE was a select group of elite agents that carried out the law the way it was meant to be. Only a few were selected as members. First, they had to work for Dartanian's legitimate business. They were observed, tested, and, if proven, they were brought into ICE.

Inner Court Executions.

ICE drew upon all assets of DSS—the computers, police, and intelligence connections. Through DSS, Alex kept track of unpunished crimes. And then, unlike the courts and the bloodied liberals, he acted upon them.

Tonight's rendezvous with the Jamaican was no accident; it was a premeditated chill.

A police lieutenant in the know quietly tipped off Dartanian to Razor Mikey's rap sheet—a dozen slasher killings, from teenagers, to winos and grandmas.

It took five nights of riding the subways before Dartanian rode the right car, before Razor stalked *him*. It took thirty seconds to send him to hell.

One

The silver van cruised down Baker Street at five o'clock in the morning. Inside were three men—and a dozen weapons. It was a warwagon, ready for the cops or a small army. Nothing but death could stop it.

Trees and late model imports lined the second block of Baker Street, giving the neighborhood an elegant, safe look. On this cool summer morning, misty and breezy under a fading blue sky, safety was an expensive illusion.

A light flashed once in the middle of the block, and the van picked up speed and headed toward the signal. It rolled over to the curb as a man dressed in black hurried out of a well-kept brownstone.

There was a human package slung over his shoulder. The legs stuck out from a light summer blanket as he silently skipped down the steps. Over his other shoulder were a travel bag and a leather purse.

In one smooth motion he threw her into the open door of the van and jumped in after her. The blanket came off as the door clicked shut behind him.

She was about twenty, wearing a red transparent nightgown.

"Nice of you to giftwrap her," Doc said, smiling as the van quietly drove off.

The man in black forced a smile. "Yeah, she's a treat, alright. I kinda hate to give her up."

The girl stirred at the sound of her lover's voice. "It's late, Jerry, I need some sleep."

"Coming up," Doc said. He lovingly removed a metallic syringe from the leather pouch strapped to his belt. Jerry held the girl's arm while Doc injected her with some peace and quiet. Last night's ludes and Doc's needle would keep her down for a while.

Doc, dressed as if he was still a reknown professional surgeon, looked fondly at the empty needle.

"Don't even think it, Doc," Jerry said. "Not yet. Wreck yourself on your own time. We haven't made the delivery yet."

"Hey, kid, I was just going to maintain. Honestly."

"Do it when the job's over. Okay?" Jerry's voice was nice and easy, full of reason, but there was another quality there. A promise that Jerry, the handsome gentle guy with the charming smile, would have Doc killed in a second if he thought the doper was losing control.

As the van's supershocks absorbed the potholes and bumps of the rundown streets, Doc and Jerry lifted the girl and tossed her on top of the plushy carpeted platform.

"Let me take a look at her," Doc said, casually sliding his hand beneath the flimsy red gown. His stroking fingers covered her well formed breast. "What's our patient's name?"

"Cindy," Jerry said. "Cindy Brooks."

"Well, Cindy, you're in good hands now," he laughed stupidly. The laugh turned into a series of uncontrolled murmuring as he ran his hands over the unconscious girl's body.

Jerry looked at Doc and wondered how long before they had to kill the silver-haired quack; he was getting too close to the edge.

He leaned back against the carpeted wall of the van. He didn't feel like talking; he was nervous. Doc kept chattering away, asking questions, crackling, and eyeing the woman on the platform.

It all went too smoothly, Jerry thought. He was still up from the adrenalin pumping through him before the grab. And nowhere to put all that energy, to spend out his nerves jangling inside.

Jerry sensed something was wrong. He couldn't pin it down. It was a flutter of doubt, a sixth sense outburst, but it faded. He looked back over the operation. Nothing was wrong; no mistakes. They had the chick and they were on their way to sell her ass.

"She comes from good stock, that's for sure," Doc said. "How'd you get hold of her?"

"She's a WASP princess looking for adventure in the big city," Jerry said.

"Well, she sure as hell found it, didn't you, honey?" Doc stroked her smooth flat belly like she was a kitten. "She won't like it, but she found all the adventure she can handle." Doc started laughing again as he pushed aside the nightgown.

Jerry got a weird feeling watching the man's hands slide over Cindy's bare skin. But why worry about that? What right did he have to complain? He was the one who conned her, the one who was about to peddle her flesh into the slave trade.

All the chicks were easy. Jerry had the looks, the lean body, the clothes, and the attitude, and the cold charm that made them all want to please him. Then he just walked right in and took them over, body and soul.

It took three weeks for Cindy to give in totally and trust him, to let him move in. Cindy Brooks, dreamy eyed, looking for success as an actress or artist, or whatever she could become in the big city. She was his, and in a short while she was going to be someone else's. For keeps.

"Come on, Doc. Save your leching for later. You'll have plenty of time for that. See if you can pry your hands off of her and help me go through her stuff."

Jerry pushed aside the travel bag that he'd packed with her clothes so it would look like she was away on a planned vacation. He opened her purse and emptied the contents on the van floor.

Besides selling her ass, they had her money, rings, and credit cards. They'd split the cash four ways and fence the rest. Whatever was in the purse was frosting on the cake.

Doc rifled her wallet. "Hell, she's loaded. Look at these." He tossed a handful of credit cards on the floor. "Hey, wait a second."

"What is it?"

Doc was excited now, practically shouting. The two men in front glanced through the curtains to see what was going on.

Doc waved her driver's license in his hand. "Take a look. I thought you said her name was Cindy Brooks." He passed the license to Jerry. "This says her name's Cindy Barrington." He grabbed a few credit cards from the floor. "These too. What the hell is going on?"

"Quiet down," Jerry said. "Lots of chicks change their names, especially actresses. It probably doesn't mean anything." He was worried though. He should have checked her out more. She could be anybody.

"Yeah," Doc said, pleased that he had something to

ride Jerry about. He had that perfect little bastard in hot water at last. "Yeah, but what if she's somebody big?"

Jerry spoke loud enough for everyone in the van to hear. "Relax. If she's somebody special, we can kill her. After we sell her ass, that is."

They settled back for the ride upstate after Doc quieted down.

The men in the front were quiet. Stu drove, nothing else. He always kept their wheels in shape. Stu had customized the van, installed hidden gunports, and tooled the engine up. He drove. He didn't talk because all he liked to talk about was cars and engines, and his partners were imbeciles when it came to car talk. Incompetents. It was up to Stu to haul their ass out of the fire time after time.

Every man in the team had a purpose. Jerry picked out the chicks, conned them, and got them ready for sale. He handled the delivery deals since he knew how to talk to those people. Fast and smooth. Doc supplied the drugs to calm the girls when it was necessary. He knew how to dose them without killing them or ruining the goods. Doc was in on the snatch; he also remained at the drop-off to help train the girls. The man in the passenger seat, whistling, looking back at the girl every now and then, and then out the window was Martin. He was the hit man. He hit rival gangs, cops, and sometimes one of the chicks they delivered, just to give the other girls a lesson.

Every man in the van would kill if it came to that, but Martin did it best. He was born to the trade. He hit with style and feeling. He was easygoing, right up to the time he offed a target.

Martin fiddled with the radio all the way up to the Catskills, trying to listen to WNEW, even in the mountains. No one argued with him about the static coming over the channel.

After two hours of driving on the New York State Thruway, they got off in the middle of the Catskills. Stu didn't slow down even when they were on the winding convoluted roads that took them deeper into the wilds.

It was resort territory with pockets of luxury carved out of the countryside. One road took you into hillbilly country; the next took you into a costly wonderland. Hotels and summer camps and festivals of every stripe catered to tourists all season long. All the stars came out to play.

It was also retreat territory. A man could build his own fortress, staff it with his own soldiers, and all the women money could buy, and live a secret existence.

The van made one last turn onto a dirt trail partially blocked by brush and overhanging elm branches. It was the back entrance and escape route, used only for special occasions.

After three-quarters of a mile, the trail turned into a smooth road that led uphill for another quartermile. An iron gate and a guardhouse stopped the van cold.

Two men in shark suits pulled open the side door of the van and climbed inside. Their drawn .45's waved hello to the occupants.

Jerry recognized the muscle and nodded.

"Just checking, man," one said. "One, two, three, four," he said, counting heads. "And there's the cheese-cake." He pointed his gun hand at the half naked girl in the back of the van. "Okay, go on up to the ga-rage." He hopped out of the van and waved them on.

A gravel road led uphill to a series of chateau-style buildings on the mountain top. It looked like the sum-mer home of a king, a Rockefeller, or a slave trader.

A manmade pond stocked with swans, gamefish,

and a dozen women in revealing swimsuits was off to the right of the compound. There, beneath a white enameled umbrella table, sat three men in casual dress, sipping coffee and watching the women.

The women were obviously cold from the brisk morning air but none of them made an effort to get out of the water. Instead of a lifeguard sitting in the ladder chair at the edge of the pond, there was a guard with an automatic rifle cradled across his lap. He looked straight at the women.

None of the women looked at the guard or at the men at the table. It was part of their training. To break the rules or displease the smiling man delicately sipping his coffee could bring a lingering depraved death.

The smiling man got up from the table as the van approached. He had the look of a rich collector about to add another priceless piece to his collection. This was Mr. Storm. He was a dark complexioned man in his early forties, broad and well-muscled. As he welcomed Jerry inside the garage, he spoke slowly with perfect diction, as though English was his second language. Mr. Storm appeared to be an Arab, but no one ever inquired about his background. It wasn't polite or healthy.

All that mattered to Jerry was that Storm was a good man to do business with. "Ah, Mr. Storm," Jerry said. He hauled out the girl with Doc's help. "I'm glad you were in the market. This one is too exquisite to give to someone else."

"Boast all you want, my friend. She does look charming. But the price remains the same."

Jerry laughed, following the swarthy man's cue. It was good to maintain the facade of friendship inside Mr. Storm's fortress. The block-shaped garage had at least three floors and sub-basements below. Jerry had seen what one of the floors was used for, and it still gave him shudders. It was the floor that Cindy would be heading for very shortly.

Stu and Martin stayed inside the van parked in the garage while Jerry and Doc carried the girl down a hall connected to another small chateau. They followed Mr. Storm into a room full of rustic comfort that would have cost at least ten grand to furnish.

, "Excuse me a moment," Mr. Storm said. "I'll be back with my half of the bargain."

When he left Jerry glared at Doc. "Remember," he hissed. "Don't say a word about the names. I'll check this out myself and find out who she is. I'll take care of everything. Just don't talk about it to our friend, huh?"

Doc smiled.

"I mean it, Doc."

Doc nodded his head but he still had an odd look about him that said he was capable of anything.

Mr. Storm came back with a brown wrapped package of fifty dollar bills that he handed to Jerry. "Here is your fee," he said. "Minus, of course, the good doctor's share. He and I shall work things out to our own satisfaction."

Jerry nodded. Storm probably supplied Doc with heroin or coke or maybe even his very own chick. It was possible, Jerry thought. Doc spent an awful lot of time out here. Maybe he owned a girl. Or maybe Storm owned Doc. Storm got his hooks into everybody he could. A junkie like Doc would be easy to control.

"Again, I thank you for your services," Storm said to Jerry, dismissing him. "And Doc, if you will wait in your quarters, I believe I'll get acquainted with our new guest. What is her name, please?"

"Cindy," Doc said.

Jerry held his breath and paused at the door.

"Cindy Brooks," Doc continued.

*   *   *

Cindy Barrington woke up in a room that reminded her of a basement. It was stark white, unfinished, and the walls seemed to close in on her. It looked just like a cell.

Her head felt stranded in unconsciousness, unwilling to lift up and look around. She opened and closed her eyes, unable to focus long enough before the pain came. The headache ripped through her in searing white light shafts of pain.

God, she thought, where did she and Jerry go last night? Whose place was this? She tried to remember what wild party had landed her here. Cindy groaned and closed her eyes. She sank her head down and remembered the dreams. Weird dreams about a van, some kind of van with other guys in it, but Jerry was there, too.

Ohhhh, God. . . . God . . . God . . . The rape! She dreamed she was raped. The memory of pain was so vivid. Her hands automatically went to her thighs. Sore. But then she was sore all over.

It was cold. Cindy reached for the blankets and found none. She was naked and shivering and her flesh was chilled from the cold blasts of air pumped into the room. Whoever owned this place had the air conditioner on too high. She would definitely mention the cold when she went down for breakfast.

The bed was so damn hard. It was a metal cot. She suddenly came up from the haze again, from the drugs that tried to reclaim her.

Where the hell was she?

Something was around her leg. Something cold. She moved her ankle and heard a clanking sound. Her neck snapped up and she saw a chain around her leg. The chain held her to the bed. A cold maddening sensation sliced through her brain.

Cindy thought she might have had an accident during the night. And they brought her to a hospital. Then she went crazy and they chained her to the bed for her own good. It was a psychiatric ward, that was it. But she was out of it now. She was safe. She pulled through. Oh, God, she couldn't wait to get out.

She shouted. Then she screamed. Finally the door opened. A silver-haired man with a doctor's bag came into the room.

"I'm okay," she said. "I snapped out of it."

"Oh? You snapped out of it, did you? Out of what?"

"The coma, or whatever it was that happened to me. I'm better now."

The doctor started laughing. "Coma?" A series of low-pitched chuckles came from his mouth. "You thought you were in a coma. That's rich. You *must* be nuts." He started laughing again.

Cindy's voice wavered. "Listen . . . Listen, I don't know who you are, but when Jerry finds out about this—"

He went into hysterics, but then he suddenly cut his laughter short. Something else commanded his attention. Her body. She blushed, tried to cover herself, but there was no way. She couldn't move away from him either. The chain only gave her a foot of space to move around.

"Yes," he said, "you are quite lovely. Such a nice ripe figure. Such pretty red hair. Mind if I touch?" He stepped closer and reached for her.

Cindy screamed. She fell backward onto the bed, still screaming as he followed her. His hands crawled over her cold naked flesh. She huddled at the far end of the bed while his fingers fluttered up and down her skin.

Cindy chattered, but couldn't stop screaming.

Then the silver-haired man slugged her in the stomach harder than she ever believed possible. It took her by surprise and doubled her over.

"Rule number one," he said. "No unnecessary screaming. No noise unless I ask for it. Understand?" He slid next to her and circled his arms around her from behind, clutching at her breasts.

The scream was automatic. "My father! My father will . . ."

The punch to her ribs was equally automatic, shutting her up except for another long gasp of pain. She could not believe what he was doing to her, that it could happen to her, the daughter of . . .

One more punch to her stomach knocked her into a crazy place, where survival was her only God. It was a place where she didn't want to talk or get hit.

His hands grabbed and scratched her skin. He held her with his hands, pinning her around her battered stomach. "Now you can talk to me," he said. "Only when I ask. Tell me about your father. Tell me your real name. Tell me everything." His voice trailed off into a gentle murmur, laced with his hideous clucking laughter.

Two

Cage Street was the safest street in New York City, day or night.

It was the site of the DSS building, a ten story marble column with mirrored windows that threw back the bright morning sun.

The building looked like it was, an imposing center of power. The force behind that center with its computers, technicians, and agents of every stripe was one man, Alex Dartanian, ruling his invisible empire from the top floor.

It was ten-thirty Monday morning, Dartanian was scanning a CIA analysis of a prospective banking client when the urgent buzzer on his desk console sounded.

Diane Cummings, his receptionist from the beginning, spoke over the intercom. "A Senator Barrington on line three, Alex. He sounds like he's cracking up."

"Got it," Alex said. A moment later he spoke into the phone. "Yes, Senator, this is Alex Dartanian speaking."

"Alex, I must talk with you . . ." The senator's voice choked off into silence. There was a lapse while he struggled to form his words, managing nothing more than a few tearful utterances.

"Senator, I can return the call if you'd like."

"Oh, God, it's about my daughter. She's, uh, she's in this . . ." Again his words trailed off and Alex listened to Senator Alan Barrington, who chaired the investigations into labor racketeering, fought for the CIA's covert abilities while Alex was still with the Company, and was seen on network television nightly fighting for a strong military . . . now he was breaking down, tearing apart in sobs and gasps and choking agony.

"Something's happened that I can't . . . I can't deal with it. Alex. I need someone to help . . ."

It was unsettling to hear Barrington, who stood for all the things Dartanian did, falling apart bit by bit. He was broken, his emotions fractured like a scared rabbit.

"Are you in town, Senator?"

"Yes. I'm staying at the Hartford Inn. Suite 310."

"I'll be right over, Senator," Dartanian said. "We can talk there, if you like."

"Yes, please."

"In half an hour." Dartanian hung up the phone and buzzed the intercom. "Diane, erase the tape of that last call. Thank you."

Thirty minutes later Dartanian was comfortably seated in the luxury suite, facing Senator Barrington, who was leaning forward in his chair, clasping his hands.

Barrington's eyes were red, his face drained white. He looked eighty instead of the young sixty he normally appeared on the Senate floor.

"Why are you so shattered?" Dartanian asked.

"I have a daughter," Senator Barrington said.

Dartanian nodded. "Yes, I recall." He remembered

the file photos of the girl and the report. She had a drunken driving violation when she was seventeen, and last year she had been involved in a drug bust. A ridiculous two joint caper that the press harped on for a solid month. "Pretty girl."

"She is. I have reason to believe that she is in serious trouble. Two sources have come to me so far, and I have to conclude that what they say is true."

"Go on, Senator," Alex said. Alex needed as much information as possible while the Senator had his composure.

"This may sound outlandish, impossible in this day and age, but I think Cindy has . . . fallen victim to a . . . sex slavery gang." His face reddened with shame and anger. "I know it's hard to believe," he continued.

"I'm familiar with them," Dartanian added. "They exist. They're well organized, ruthless, and there's little chance of recovery in these cases—"

"Dammit!" the senator thundered as he leaped from his chair. "Dammit, how in the hell can they operate in this country!"

"We both know the answer," Dartanian said. "In our own ways, we both are trying to correct that problem. I was going to say that the chances of recovery are slim by conventional means. You know my background. You know I'll get it done."

Senator Barrington paced the floor, reaching out for assurance. "Yes, I know if it's possible, you can come through. But there's always a chance for the worst . . ."

"Naturally," Dartanian said. "But we can't operate on that assumption. Otherwise we're defeated before we begin. Now, if you will give me all the details . . ."

It took some time before Senator Barrington got the complete story out. Then, with Dartanian's probing, he was able to put together a chronology of what happened.

One of Barrington's colleagues, a senator from Massachusetts, was the first to approach him with the news. The senator had always been surrounded in controversy and suppressed scandal. Barrington wouldn't name him unless it was absolutely vital. But the colleague had definitely been around. A womanizer, a well known debaucher, and a powerful influence in the Senate.

He had seen Barrington's daughter, or someone who looked very much like her, at a weekend bash on Martha's Vineyard. The girl, a redhead like Cindy, had been performing in a live sex show that one of the senator's cronies had imported which included a dozen other call girls.

"This colleague of yours," Dartanian said. "He knew Cindy well enough to identify her?"

"A good chance," Barrington responded. "We've met socially a few times. While the families mingled, he and I conducted some business. His family is very decent, although his personal life is a shambles."

"And he volunteered this information to you?" Dartanian said.

"Yes. The bastard was gloating. First he described the girl, then her performance, and then said he was positive it was Cindy. When he expressed interest in meeting her, the girl was taken away suddenly."

Barrington hadn't heard from Cindy in some time and when he checked out her place on Baker Street, she hadn't been seen for days. He waited another couple of days just in case. Cindy had been known to take off for holidays. Finally he began to believe that she might be mixed up in something sordid.

Then the call came.

The man on the phone sounded nervous, and a bit odd, like he wasn't in good emotional shape. He asked about Barrington's daughter. Barrington thought it was a crank. And then the man mentioned that Cindy was in the hands of a slave ring. He told Barrington to collect fifty thousand dollars if he ever wanted to see her again. The caller said he would call back the next day with more details. He threatened the girl's death if the senator went to the police.

"And?" Dartanian asked.

"Not another word from him. He never called back. And here I am with you. I didn't call the police or to the FBI. All I could think of was you, and how you reacted at that intelligence hearing. Believe me, I've followed your career ever since you told the Texas senator to take his head out of his ass and stop stroking the Soviets."

Dartanian smiled thinly. He remembered the hearing when every senator—except Barrington—was out to castrate the CIA in order to get a few more votes.

"Yes," Dartanian said. "That was televised, wasn't it? I resigned shortly after that. Thanks to a few of your colleagues."

Senator Barrington shook his head. "Those are the very same bastards now clamoring for a stronger CIA. Anyway the wind blows for those shylocks."

I'll need some photos," Dartanian said. He wrote a list of Cindy's friends that Barrington was aware of. The places she hung out and what type of life she led.

"She wanted to be an actress. But she really just needed the time to grow up. Now maybe she won't have the chance to . . . I was going to support her for a year or two until she came to her senses, and then I was going to help her find a real career."

"Any special guy in her life?" Dartanian asked.

"No. She was popular. A lot of dates. A lot of names . . . Wait. She called me about a month ago, or six weeks, I forget. And she mentioned some guy she was going out with that night . . . Damn, I can't remember his name."

"Let me know if it comes to you, Senator," Dartanian said. "In the meantime we'll take a run through the jungle."

At DSS headquarters, Dartanian summoned the available intelligence about the sex slavery business. There was a good deal of general information, but nothing concrete.

Interpol had files on international connections, and dealers who peddled drugs, arms, and bodies, but they were usually after the fact. The deals had already gone down and the dealers were spread out, lying low.

Until the next time.

And the next.

It was an endless parade of human misery and there seemed little chance of stopping it.

Interpol continually made recommendations to the United Nations about how to stop the flow of international traffic in women—recommendations the United Nations continually ignored.

A major part of the problem was that more than forty countries in the United Nations still condoned slavery, although in an unofficial fashion. The international antislavery conventions were still not ratified by fifty member states of the UN.

Without international cooperation, Interpol was a toothless paper tiger.

Afghanistan was a major supplier of narcotics and women. So was Thailand. Hong Kong was the world capital of flesh for sale. The list included Venezuela, Brazil, Paraguay, France, and even the United States, especially in New York City.

Dartanian checked CIA dossiers and local police

files, getting names involved on the periphery of the sex slave trade. Pimps and dealers. It was the same story.

The gangs kept popping out, making their hits, then disappearing, like rats hiding in the darkness of fear. No one liked to talk about it.

The slavers operated in several ways. There were the newspaper ads for overseas employment, the ads for artistic talent—hostesses and dancers who were forced into slavery step by step—and there was the old method of kidnapping.

Fear, punishment, drugs, and mind control techniques were employed on the women to keep them totally submissive to their captors. They were remade into living dolls who couldn't think or speak for themselves. It could mean death.

It was the American way, Dartanian thought. Money could buy anything, the ultimate consumer society. There would always be a market for human suffering, and those willing to supply it.

It was the same with the cults that operated so blatantly across the country, making their bucks from shattered minds. At times America looked like one big hustlers' convention to Dartanian; the creeps fleeced and preyed on those who played by the rules.

The police couldn't stop it. The government couldn't and they would not stop the selling the American spirit.

It was up to private sources and individuals who knew when it was time to take a stand.

It was up to men like Alex Dartanian and the men of ICE.

Right now the only way to get Senator Barrington's daughter back was to play the same game the creeps were, but with one difference. Dartanian and his men would be harder and meaner and deadlier than the opposition. Dartanian would use his best weapons, Mick Porter and Sin Simara.

ICE was going hunting with all the tools that Dartanian's DSS organization could offer. ICE was going to strike hard and loud, like the shrieking of the American spirit coming back from the grave.

Three

Benny Madeira was strutting on top of the world when he left his pub on Columbus Avenue at 3 A.M. Business was good now that Benny's Pub had been "discovered" by the night-life crowd. Good food, drink, entertainment, and big payoffs to the society columnists insured the discovery. Of course the payoffs were accompanied by a few well chosen threats.

Benny's place was packed with actresses, writers, and fashion flies. They had money to burn, Benny made sure they had the chance. He had a discreet line of girls working the joint, along with a couple of Ivy League drug dealers. It wasn't called high society for nothing.

Yeah, he thought, strolling down the street to his Porsche, yeah, he had it made.

He had money, beautiful women, and all the comfort a man could ask for. He had respect in the legit world. A success. There was no trace of his cheap hood origins in the white suit, black shirt, and white tie, tailored to the lean body that worked out three times a week at the health club.

Things were alright for Benny Madeira. They kept on being alright until he got hit by the truck—Mick Porter's ham-sized fist thudding into Madeira's kidney. The blow stunned, silenced, and turned him into a rag doll that Mick easily tossed into a dark alley between two fashionable watering holes.

Madeira cursed as he rolled down the alley, staining his white suit with grime.

"Don't turn around," Mick said. "Just give me some answers."

"You're making a big mistake, chump," Madeira said. "I got some heavy connections."

"Yeah?" Mick said. "Well let's hope those connections include a coupla gravediggers. That's all you're gonna need unless you get real polite."

The white-suited hood had time to recover by now. He balanced himself on his hands, breathed deeply, and got ready to turn and fight.

Madeira scrambled to his feet, pulled back his right hand for a punch, and stopped in midswing—the moment he saw the shadowy giant silhouetted against the light from the faraway street. The black clad hulk had a hood over his face.

"Don't stop on account of me," Mick Porter said, laughing. "Go on, tough guy, do what you were about to do."

"I'm no fool," Madeira said. "But in my day I put down a lot of dudes bigger than you, pal."

"Your day's over, *pal.*"

Madeira brushed off the sleeves of his suit. "Okay, what is it? What do you want? Money?"

The first punch caught him in the face; the next three tore apart his upper body, ripping and crashing through muscle. The last punch rang bells in his ears that he usually only heard on Sunday mornings.

Madeira crumpled to the ground.

"Sorry," Mick said. "I never could handle insults too well."

The man groaned as Mick picked him up by the collar of his now tattered suit and pushed him face against the brick wall. "Now, you just give me some information, and I'll be on my way."

Madeira spit blood and swore. "I don't talk to no one, pal!"

Wham! The same kidney exploded with another hard-knuckled punch. "Four other guys gave me the same routine tonight," Mick said. "Right now they're probably being scraped into a body bag." Wham! He punched him again. "Do we understand one another?"

Madeira groaned.

"No one has to know, pal. This is between you and me. Give me what I want and I'll go away. If not, I'll waste you. Right here and now. It doesn't matter to me at all."

Madeira nodded his head and slumped against the wall. "What's it about . . . What do you want?"

"Chicks for sale, man," Mick said. "Slaving. I want the name of a young guy, smooth talking, a slick little hustler that's working your club and a few others. You know, the sleaze set."

When slaving was mentioned, Benny Madeira stiffened. Once he gave a name, it would lead to another, and still another, all the way to where a man could get killed for mentioning the wrong name.

Mick ran down all the names and places where Cindy was seen, all the faces, and then he asked for the name of the man fitting the description of the girl's latest lover.

"No more time," Mick said. "You know what I want.

You know what I'll do to get it." He reached up with his left hand and circled Madeira's neck. His strong fingers began closing, crushing his windpipe.

Madeira flailed against the wall, choked, sputtered, and tried to kick Mick back. He knew that nothing could stop death but a name.

"Jerry . . . Jerry Cornell is working the joints, scoring the chicks." He was so happy to be breathing again that he spilled everything he knew.

Madeira was still talking when Mick Porter turned and left the alley. He had the name. Jerry Cornell. It checked out with all the other creeps that Mick visited. Jerry kept coming up in conversation whenever pressure was applied.

Mick walked two blocks to his silver BMW and tossed the black hood into the back seat. Most likely he wasn't going to be dressing up again tonight.

Dartanian had them putting on the heat. It was the only way to collect information in a hurry. During the day, DSS agents combed the neighborhood haunts of Cindy Brooks or Cindy Barrington. Hardly anyone knew her as Barrington. She and her father agreed a long time ago that if she went under the name of Brooks there would be less chance of scandal. She was too tempting a target to go around as Cindy Barrington. Everyone loved taking cheap shots at the senator's daughter.

The information came in bit by bit. The names of pimps and possible traders were whispered when money flashed, or when DSS men put the heat on. Their informers always had a bust or two hanging over their heads, and it was easy enough to pull them in for the cops—unless they cooperated.

And they did cooperate. DSS had turned the underworld into one big happy family.

This was the conventional part of the assignment.

At night ICE was unleashed and Mick Porter went hunting. He traveled from bar to bar, the shady haunts that most men thought twice about entering. But no one ever bothered Mick Porter. He had a certain aura about him. He was six-foot-four an ex-linebacker, ex-Special Forces agent.

He was getting known on the scene, soaking up the atmosphere. And then, after hours, he put on the hood. Not only did it keep his face hidden, but it put fear into his interviewees.

At four in the morning, he drove back to DSS head-quarters to make his report. Mick went over the night's activities. He couldn't help laughing to himself. All his threats and talk came straight from spy movies, gang-ster flicks. Besides gadgets and guns, women and wine, gangster movies were Mick's great passion. Many mornings he had "television eyes" from watching the tube all night.

The funny part about it was that it worked. The tough guy talk worked. It was the only language that hoods like Benny Madeira understood.

On Wednesday afternoon Dartanian called a war council. While a hazy 100° day baked the city, he sat in his air-conditioned office, alert and cool, planning the destruction of Jerry Cornell.

Seated across from his computer consoled desk were Mick Porter and Sin Simara. Mick was wearing a three hundred dollar suit and resting at his feet was a leather suitcase containing his favorite submachine pistol—the Ingram M10. It fired 1000 rounds in sixty seconds. The night scope and silencer made it a 24-hour guardian angel.

Mick looked like a businessman. All business.

Sitting next to him in loose fitting black pants and a black v-neck t-shirt, all Sin Simara had as weapons

were his slender hands, his bony feet, and his decep-
tive small frame. Those weapons were more than
enough.

The slim Japanese man had been born into the
martial arts. His family considered the practice and
discipline as natural as breathing. Ever since childhood,
Sin had been taught to take the next step, learn the
next system, and finally create his own style. One
principle guided Sin. In his culture man was always a
student, no matter how old or how skilled. As a result,
Sin Simara, student and master, was never satisfied
with his abilities. He kept training, learning, growing,
and hoping to transcend human limitations.

To Mick Porter, Sin had already transcended the
human condition. He considered Sin an alien whose
one joy in life was to kick Mick Porter's ass every
chance he could under the guise of training.

The two of them bickered constantly, more so when
they were on ICE. It helped relieve the tensions and
keep them happy.

Mick felt that Sin Simara spent one third of his time
in training, another third meditating, and the remaining
third charming women out of their skins.

"It's going to take a day or two before we jump into
this all the way," Dartanian said.

"Perhaps we should use the time to train," Sin
Simara said, smiling innocently at Mick Porter.

"No thanks," Mick said. "I'd rather bang my head
against the wall."

"Anything to improve your looks, eh?" Sin said.

Dartanian worked his briefing in and out of their
jiving. He was used to it and never thought of trying to
stop it. Mick and Sin were the best army a man could
have and they could play it any way they wanted to.
There was no sense in spoiling such a good relationship.

Although Dartanian was their superior, they were all equal, part of a small brotherhood that had fought side by side for years.

"What's the script?" Mick asked.

"Two ways. Either I work my way in as part of Jerry's gang—assuming that he is the one that hit Cindy Barrington—or I take him over and become the new man in town."

Sin Simara, who took great pains to be 100% Americanized, leaned forward in his chair and said, "What's my gig, man? We have Mick for the stooge, the muscle, we have you for the underground man, and me, what's there for me?"

"I don't want to expose you too much, Sin," Dartanian said. "For now you can lay back, make a few quiet hits if we need to. Later, if all goes well, I'll bring you into the works as my Japanese connection."

Sin nodded his head and clasped his fingers together into a steeple and worried his Rhett Butler mustache. "Good," he said. "I see no problem in getting oriented."

Mick groaned at the pun. "Yeah, well if anyone was ever good at Shanghaing a chick, it's you."

Sin Simara hissed lightly and formed both hands into eagle claws. "Sure you don't want to train for a while?"

Dartanian finished laying out a capsule of all their intelligence gatherings—the names, bars, money involved in flesh sales—just so Mick and Sin could play their parts when the time came.

If all went well, Jerry Cornell would be hungry for more bucks and surface at his local haunts. That time was going to come real soon.

Jerry Cornell, most likely using an alias since his name didn't come up on any of the computers, was last seen about a week ago. He usually laid low for that amount of time and then came back to the surface. He was like the others in the street scene. They couldn't stay away from it long enough to be safe. They all had to bask in the wormy glory of the underground set, the hang-around guys and the hang-around chicks.

With a half dozen DSS men quietly looking through the bars and clubs that made up Jerry's scene, he was going to be spotted right away.

And then Alex Dartanian was going to make his move, and keep making it until he chopped his way through the jungle and returned with one young, vulnerable Cindy Barrington.

Dead or alive. If she was dead, she was going to have lots of company.

On his way out Dartanian's office, Sin Simara turned and said, "One thing. What if this Jerry character isn't our man. What if we're climbing up the wrong tree?"

"Simple," Dartanian said. "We burn down the forest."

---------------------- *Four* ----------------------

Dartanian wore faded jeans and a denim shirt with the sleeves rolled up to his elbows as he sat around the High Hat, pretending to be slightly drunk. His blonde hair was dyed black and his mustache was off. Tinted glasses covered his 20/20 eyes. He looked like a dozen other hang-around guys scouting for action.

Three seats down from him, leaning over the cigarette scarred mahogany bar, was Jerry Cornell. Parked next to him was a short skirted barmaid hoping for a ride.

No doubt about it, Dartanian thought. The kid did have an effect on women, all ages, sizes, and kinds.

It was the third night in a row Dartanian had seen Jerry in the High Hat. In that time they had talked bar talk, bought each other a few drinks, and shot some pool.

A lazy jazz trio walked through some slinky standards in a corner of the bar while hostesses in black uniforms with deep dip bodices took orders and made after hours arrangements. It was a place to unwind after a dishonest day's work.

When the barmaid left Jerry's side, Dartanian motioned him to join him. They talked through three drinks with Jerry tossing his whiskey down straight, getting glassy eyed and full of fire.

"Let's talk," Dartanian said.

"I thought we were talking," Jerry said, laughing.

"Business," Dartanian said. "Let's talk some business."

Jerry, the wise young man about town, nodded and followed Dartanian to a table.

"Look, kid," Dartanian began. "I usually got plenty of work, but I'm new on the set and a bit thin in the wallet."

"What's your line of work?" Jerry asked. "And why come to me?"

"Hey, we're in the same line. Women. And I come to you because you're the man to come to."

"Who says?" Jerry was noncommital, but not too surprised. Nearly everyone on the scene knew who to come to for those special services.

"I been told," Dartanian said. "But I don't like to give out names. Know?"

Jerry nodded and accepted another shot of whiskey.

They talked a bit more, with Jerry never denying or confirming that he was in the business Dartanian claimed. Jerry threw out a few probes between drinks.

"Where'd you come from, anyhow?"

"Montreal," Dartanian answered. "Things got hot. There was a bust stretching clear down to Plattsburgh, and I had to split." Everything he said about the bust was true. There had been a big bust, with dozens of dealers and border crossers going down. And there had been some killings.

Jerry was thinking and Dartanian could tell that he

liked what he heard. Either he already knew about the Montreal bust, or knew that he could check it out simple enough.

"What'd you do?" Jerry said.

"Let's just say that I helped a few souls on their way to hell. They sang a bit too loud."

"So that's your talent, huh?"

"One of them, kid. I got more. Hell, I had my own chick farm once and I want it again. But I gotta start someplace. And that's why I'm talking to you."

Jerry enjoyed the conversation. It was splashed all over his clear blue eyes that he liked being the man to see and do business with.

"Suppose I am what you think?" Jerry said. "What makes you think I can take somebody new on? If the demand ain't there, it just ain't there, you know?"

"Hell with that attitude," Dartanian said. "I can dig up all the customers we need. I know a sonofabitch Turk that's always in the market. I know a few pipelines to London, Japan, Thailand, man, I can expand you wherever you want to go, but to start with I'll turn you on to the Turk."

"Too late, man," Jerry said. "Your Turk named Storm?"

"Yeah," Dartanian said. "Storm." That confirmed his guess about Storm being one more link in the chain leading to Cindy Barrington.

The same barmaid came over, fluttering around Jerry, patting him, wondering if she won the lottery. Jerry looked at her big tits in her laced top. "Go away, baby," he said. "Maybe later." She pouted and took off.

Dartanian eyed the tightly packed barmaid sailing away, a vision of black fishnet stockings and curves. "You get all the chicks you want, don't you?" he said.

Jerry looked around the bar, woman to woman.

"Yeah. Pick a girl, any girl. I can get her for you wholesale." He laughed and tossed down one more shot of whiskey.

"You know your business, I know mine," Dartanian said.

"Do you?" Jerry leaned forward. "A lot of guys talk like you. A lot of it's total shit. So how do I know?"

Dartanian looked around the bar and saw hard cases of every type. "Pick a guy," he said. "Any guy."

The handsome, boyish slaver took a long deliberate look around the bar. His eyes finally rested on the bouncer, a man in his forties who'd been playing pool all night. His zebra-striped tank top showed beyond doubt that he was a weight lifter. He was muscled to his shaved gleaming bald head. A concrete block with eyes.

"Hey, Cordy!" Jerry shouted. "This guy says you're a mongoloid!"

All the chatter in the bar stopped at once. The jazz trio kicked down low, bass and piano in slow motion, while the drummer brushed away, oblivious to the scene in front of him.

The bouncer smiled, rapped the pool cue on the edge of the table to smoke away some chalk, and slowly made his shot. He softly tapped the five ball into the corner pocket, then laid down his stick across the table.

As he headed towards Dartanian, the other tables quickly emptied. Jerry moved right with them.

Cordy stopped three feet away from the table and glared at Dartanian.

"That right?" Cordy said. "You called me a mongoloid?"

"I didn't say a word."

Dartanian heard a few mutters from the crowd, a few sighs that he was backing down.

"I thought so," Cordy said, as he turned and walked away.

"Mongoloid," Dartanian said.

This time the bald man came fast. He knocked over a table and two chairs on his way to Dartanian.

Dartanian moved forward to meet him, throwing Cordy off guard. Most people simply ran. Even as the bouncer was pulling back his hand for a club-like swing, Dartanian closed the gap. His left hand shot straight up, the open palm clicking Cordy's jaws together, fingers clawing into his lips.

Cordy bellowed and swung wildly with his left hand, hammering into Dartanian's rib, spitting fire into his suddenly choked lungs.

Instinct raised Dartanian's knee into the solid mass now circling him for a bear hug. Once, twice, he kneed towards his groin, finding it the second time.

The bouncer roared and loosened his grip. His eyes were wet from the pain as he stepped back. He held his arms in front of him in a wrestler's stance, inching towards Dartanian.

He knew the weight would crush him if Cordy got close a second time. Dartanian waited until the bouncer took another step. Then he snapped out a side thrust kick to the thigh, wrenching deep into the muscle. Cordy staggered and dropped his head for a split second.

Dartanian's foot continued upward and snapped into Cordy's bleeding mouth. Cordy reeled backwards and took calculated steps until he was at the pool table. He grabbed the cue stick and held it by the thin end with both hands. He charged Dartanian and swung the stick like a baseball bat. It whistled through the air straight for his chest.

Dartanian ducked low and made a circle block with his right hand, catching the stick and pulling it forward.

At the same time his left hand pulled out a black Gerber fighting knife from his belt. As Cordy lost his balance and followed the cue stick, Dartanian sliced him from wrist to shoulder.

A bright red glowing line spread all over Cordy's arm as he sprawled onto the floor.

It was the only way to end the fight without killing him, or getting killed. Dartanian wiped the knife on his jeans, sheathed it, and shouted to Jerry. "Come on, kid, get me out of here."

Jerry stared at Cordy, then at Dartanian, and ran after him, spilling out of the High Hat onto the street. "This way," he yelled to Dartanian. Dartanian stopped dead in his tracks, turned and then caught up with Jerry just as he leaped into a gleaming white Firebird Trans Am.

They drove off in a loud screech of tires and thirty seconds later were out of the neighborhood.

"Well?" Dartanian said, five minutes later when they were cruising at a nice safe speed.

"Well, what?"

"Come on, kid. You saw my work back there. I made you an offer and now you either accept it or we split. One thing, baby, it's a lot safer having me on your side instead of the competition's."

"Yeah," Jerry said. "Sure it is. But you move too fast. In a little while you'll probably take me over."

Dartanian smiled. "The thought crossed my mind. But . . . if I do, you'll make a lot more bread than you are now. You can bet your ass on that."

Jerry nodded. Dartanian had already proven that he could deliver whatever he promised. "Okay. You're in. Not because you scare me—you do—it's because I need you. One of my crew hasn't been seen around lately. He's an undependable bastard, a goddam hophead . . . Ah, never mind that. He's out of the picture one way or the other."

"Great," Dartanian said. "When do we go to work?" He settled back into the soft white leather seat and relaxed.

"Soon," Jerry promised. "Real soon. I got something special coming up. Right up your alley." He dropped Dartanian off in the East Village and made arrangements to pick him up two days later.

"Name the place," Jerry said.

"The High Hat," Dartanian said. "I like the atmosphere."

Jerry mumbled something about psychotics and then roared off. Dartanian glanced at the license plate but knew it was no use. The Firebird was probably stolen. The kid grinded too many gears to be used to the wheels. It was new to him. Besides, Dartanian thought, the kid was too smart to drive around for long in something so recognizable.

Doc crashed in a 42nd Street hotel, coming out of his soft dreams only long enough to go out and score again. It kept his mind off things. It kept his mind off Storm, the bastard, who was calling in his chips. Since Doc didn't have any chips to spare that meant he was owned by Storm for the rest of his life. For services rendered . . . the pure heroin, the even purer girls . . .

Now, unless he came up with enough cash to cancel his debt, Doc was going to be forced into dealing, carrying, and becoming a mule for the greedy bastard after all that Doc did for him.

Still, there was always hope. Each time the needle went in there was hope.

Besides, there was that girl, yeah, that last girl. She was a goldmine. A rich senator's daughter. As Doc waltzed around Eighth Avenue, picking his way through the small time dealers—shades of things to come for him—he thought how nice it would be to follow through.

He remembered the phone call he had made directly to Senator Barrington and how powerful he felt. The senator had treated him with respect, the respect Doc had received years ago.

Follow through . . . Follow through. The last time he spoke to Barrington he told him to have fifty grand ready if he wanted to see his daughter again. But he didn't have the nerve to follow through until now. Storm's threats and heroin's eternal twilight gave him the nerve.

There would be time for that later. First, he had to check out some peep shows and the window shows were you could make contact with the ladies.

It was paradise for Doc as the day blended into night and all the street girls came out to do their stuff and he was with one at his hotel, in his comfortable room, doing what he could, like the other clients at the Dixie.

Doc didn't sleep much. He was like a pinball shot against the cushions, travelling up to Ninth and 42nd, cruising Twelfth, and then making the whole circuit again. He hung around 47th Street, planning tomorrow's deal. He had it all mapped out, the phone booths, coffee shops, and the whole path of the ransom drop.

Sometimes in the middle of the night, he dug out the number that Cindy had revealed to him, and he had called. He got some respect because the Senator wanted to listen to him.

Well tomorrow, he was going to have more than respect. He was going to get some cash.

"Where you been?" Jerry roughed him up a bit, pushing him towards the window of the cigarette store midway between Ninth and Tenth.

"Hey, relax, relax!" Doc said, in a high but soothing voice. "It's all under control."

"The hell it is, man. Your eyes look like solid glass."

Doc shook his head. "Just maintaining, man, right to that point, and no more. You know me."

Jerry held himself in check. It was daylight and there were some street people around, low down types who would testify against their mother if it meant an extra dollar. Lowlifes just like Doc. Used up, ready for the trash bin.

"I been looking for you," Jerry said. "Been around your place three nights in a row."

"Count me out," Doc said.

"What?"

"Count me out. I got, uh, I got a job, yeah, at a clinic. I'm going straight. Cleaning up." Doc started to walk away in his rumpled clothes, the slow fade of a junkie trying to act straight, or a drunk trying to walk with dignity. Jerry watched him head to the next corner and then he got back into the Firebird.

He followed Doc for a couple minutes, then double-parked and got out on foot. He kept with the shambles of a man for another half hour as Doc made aimless detours and stops until he came to a phone booth on a deserted street corner. It was hot and blinding and everybody was trying to stay out of the sun.

Jerry stayed behind Doc and listened, his ear against the glass booth. After thirty seconds he heard a name that stabbed a blade of fear into his heart.

"Senator Barrington," Doc said, "this will be the last call. If you want to see your daughter alive you will follow the last message I left in the phone booth and make the drop here. And I hope, for your daughter's sake, that you came alone . . ."

Oh God, Jerry thought, whipping open the door to the booth. Doc. Crazy Doc was doing a ransom stunt, some half baked plan he saw on TV once, and, Barrington . . . Senator Barrington! Jerry had found nothing on her, but Doc had. He had held out, and all of them would be going down the river. His idiot ransom demand. He'd be caught and spill it all . . .

A split second after he opened the booth door, Jerry wrapped the metallic phone cord around Doc's neck, tightened it, twisted it, and then pushed down on Doc's head. He snapped his neck and then, as Doc sank to the floor of the booth, Jerry swung the phone just to make sure. Once, twice, three times he bashed the silver hair with the receiver. Then he ran for it. Whoever was coming to make the drop wasn't going to be far away.

Sin Simara rapped sharply on the door leading from Dartanian's DSS office into a separate apartment. It was spartanly furnished, but comfortable enough for those 24-hour cases that kept him chained to the job. Dartanian shouted and Sin went inside.

Dartanian was brushing his hair, checking out the heavy black dye, getting ready for his rendezvous with Jerry.

"Looks like your boy's the one we want for sure," Sin said.

"Yeah?" Dartanian said. He continued to look at the street thug face taking shape in the mirror before him.

"It's the ransom gig," Sin Simara said. "We got a series of calls, all of them fitting the make of a slightly cracked dude, just like the first time. He rang us from phone booths, coffee shops, and joints all around the Deuce. We were all set to make the drop and nail him, and then his last call was cut short."

Dartanian looked at Sin with a question in his eyes.

"The dude was killed," Sin explained. "Suffocated, with a fractured skull to boot. His prints make him a top surgeon at one time. Lotta pressure, drugs, and finally a dozen malpractice suits sent him down the road. He's been on the needle for years."

"How's that tie him to Jerry?" Dartanian asked. "It could have been his own action. He might have nabbed Cindy alone."

"No way. He was a terminal junkie, always in a fog. And besides, I got some evidence." The slender Japanese security man handed Dartanian a fresh print.

Dartanian looked at the picture and saw a silver-haired man sprawled out on the sidewalk in front of a phone booth. His left sleeve was rolled up and his forearm was covered with bloody scratches.

Then Sin handed him another photograph, a blow-up of the forearm. "He carved a message with his syringe, right into his arm. It says Jerry. He named his murderer, plain as day."

It was a blood scarred scrawl. The first few letters looked like they read J . . . E . . . R . . . the rest was too rough to make out. "Maybe it says Jerry," Dartanian said. "It's not all that clear."

"That proves it," Sin said, smiling. "You ever know a doctor with good handwriting?"

"Good work," Dartanian said. "Jerry is our boy. I've been having those kind of feelings all along. The vicious little bastard. He doesn't look like a killer, though. Lady killer, yeah, but not an executioner . . ."

Three hours later Jerry still didn't look like a killer when he picked Dartanian up in front of the High Hat. He wore a white shirt with onyx links and knife creased slacks. Jerry looked like he was ready for a night on the town.

He was driving a 1975 Ford sedan. It was white with rust gutted doors.

"See you got rid of the pussy wagon," Dartanian said.

"Yeah, it was getting too hot. Scorched my fingers, man." Jerry laughed without meaning it and didn't say another word until they reached their destination. He had a lot on his mind and it showed.

The Ford whipped through Manhattan to the upper 20's, an area getting known as Little India. There were plenty of saris and culture shock in the neighborhood. Jerry pulled up to a brick-faced garage on a side street and honked twice.

A moment later a wide green metal shuttered door rolled up and Jerry rolled the Ford inside. He pulled over to the right and parked on top of an oily lift.

"Come on and meet the gang," Jerry said.

Dartanian followed him over to a freshly painted green van. It was a drab color that made the van look old, but up close Dartanian saw that it was in perfect condition.

Jerry introduced the balding thirtyish man tinkering with the engine as Stu. "Yup," Stu said. He nodded briefly and then went back to work.

Martin sat in the passenger seat with his long legs hanging out the open door. He was smoking a cigarette and listening to the van radio. He was a hard guy with tricks in his eyes. Eyes that said he knew something that the rest of the world didn't. He gave Dartanian a stare that would have made a normal man shiver.

Dartanian looked through him like he wasn't there. He kept both hands in his windbreaker and acted bored.

Jerry introduced Dartanian by his street alias. "This is Lex Daniels," he said. "He's taking Doc's place. He's a hell of a hitter."

"He don't look like a hit man to me," Martin said and threw away his cigarette.

Before the butt hit the floor Dartanian leaped forward and grabbed Martin. He twisted his collar taut and pushed him inside the van until the back of his head tilted over the chrome gearbox. One second later Dartanian jabbed his M61 Skorpion machine pistol into Martin's neck.

With the thin wire stock folded over the barrel the Skorpion looked coiled and ready to sting. Dartanian dug the barrel into Martin's windpipe.

"This number can do 700 rounds a minute. How'd you like a couple seconds' worth?"

Martin shook his head no. The eyes that tried to stare Dartanian down a few moments ago spoke another language now. Those eyes said that Martin made a dreadful mistake and he meant no offense and he would like to go on living if that was alright with Dartanian.

"Cool down," Jerry said.

"Yeah, man," Stu said. "Not in the van. I just cleaned the carpet."

Both men talked like it was a game that could be laughed off. They knew that this man with the cold blue eyes was capable of pulling the trigger. Martin knew it the hardest.

Dartanian smiled and said, "Maybe some other time." He released Martin and stepped back. Martin slid off the seat and landed on his feet outside the van. He straightened himself out and tried to save face. The tricky eyes came back.

"I was just checking you out," Martin said. "Had to see if you got the right stuff. Hell, you'd do the same."

"I'd do it right," Dartanian said. He waved the Skorpion over Martin's chest like he was hungry to empty the curved twenty round clip before tucking it back into the shoulder holster beneath his unzipped windbreaker.

"Told you he was a psycho," Jerry said. "The man belongs."

The man known to them as Lex Daniels definitely belonged. It was a skill that Dartanian acquired over the years. Without the ability to walk into any situation and immediately make his presence known as a 'right' guy, Dartanian would have been wasted years ago.

These guys considered themselves slick and mean and quick. Dartanian showed them within one minute that he was a major league hitter. He played by their rules. Might made right.

"What the hell, no hard feelings, right?" Dartanian said.

"Right," Martin lied.

Dartanian pretended to loosen up with his new pals and drank a few beers with them. While they talked and joked he listened to the names that came up. He wanted to climb up the chain that led to Cindy Barrington and these men were the links.

As they sat around the garage with the van radio blasting and the beers from the cooler coming faster and faster, Dartanian looked forward to the time when these buddies would find out just how much of a hitman he was.

Then they would be missing links.

Five

The moon-lit pimp bar on Trevor Street was a horror show but Dartanian pretended to like it. The Spotlight Bar was Jerry's second home, and he wanted to share it with his new partner.

Inside it was dark at three o'clock in the afternoon, a cocoon for night people. The front windows were tinted black, like sunglasses, to filter out the daytime world. The pimps were vampires when it came to daylight. They worked best in darkness, they could keep their secrets hidden from the straights.

Dartanian took advantage of the situation. Soon Jerry was drinking and talking and bragging and it didn't take much to steer him in the right direction. Night after night Dartanian collected names, seeming to act disinterested, and gradually he put together the package Jerry was selling. He didn't probe too hard so Jerry wouldn't pick up on all of the questioning, but he still managed to figure out the probable links of the slave chain.

There were times when Dartanian had to fight to

keep a smile on his face. Part of pimp life was being seen with the best women, the best threads, and the best wheels. Another part was showing their power.

One night a pimp named Chandler put on a show for Jerry and Dartanian. He snapped his fingers and a blonde sitting quietly at the bar came over to their booth. She was tall and had a haughty look. High society and a voluptuous body were wrapped in a white silk dress.

"This week's model comes straight off the cover of a dozen fashion magazines. Turn around, Honey."

The blonde pivoted and then posed with her hand on her hip. She turned her head slightly over her shoulder.

Chandler snapped his fingers again. Honey turned her body, her breasts making a striking profile, her hand testing the silkiness of her hip. He snapped his fingers several more times, and each time the woman struck a dramatic pose. Most women would have looked ridiculous, but this one carried it off because she had been a professional model, as Chandler boasted.

Dartanian appreciated her beauty, but there was a coldness in her eyes. She was physically stunning but little more than an automaton. She had been crushed by something that had her totally under control.

The pimp put her through the paces, making her strike pose after pose, making her kneel at their table, making her beg like a dog to stand up again. Chandler laughed and sent her away with a slap on her ass. The woman hadn't said a word. The only emotion that passed on her face was fear. She was used to being hit.

He wondered what a gorgeous woman like that was doing with a creep like Chandler. Why did she stay with him? Dartanian knew there was a reason. The pimps always got their hooks into their women and never let go. Like the slavers.

"Nice," Jerry said. "How did you land her?"

"Like I said. She used to be on the cover of all them women magazines. Top-notch. Top dollar, too. She still fetches ransom for her services, which I manage, of course."

"She's a prize, man," Jerry said. "But how?"

Chandler smiled. He bit his capped teeth down on a sword swizzle stick and then decided to let them in on his secret. "She had a kid. It took time to get her shape back, man, and she was out. They didn't want her. And the bucks didn't come in and she didn't have a way to live. Plus she had a little kid, and what was she to do?"

Jerry smiled. "Enter the prince."

"That's right. Here she was thinking nobody wanted her and then I come along, and she thinks we're gonna get married, and then I ease her into it, you know? But she didn't like the life and she wanted out, naturally. But there was the kid. Hell, I took care of him. I paid the babysitter, bought the clothes, found a place to keep him, and keep him I did." The pimp laughed. "She doesn't see her boy unless I say so. That makes for one well-trained lady."

Chandler sat back in the booth, proud of his cleverness. Dartanian wanted to reach out and break his neck. The man had just displayed his latest possession like she was a pair of shoes he was breaking in.

Dartanian thought about the boy and the life ahead for him, raised by a trashbag like Chandler. He thought about the model and how she had to hope that she and her kid could get away someday.

"Where you keeping her?" Dartanian said.

"Interested, huh? You got good taste. She's staying at my place, man. Stop by for a visit sometime."

"I'll do that," Dartanian said. *Count on it.* He kept up the chatter with Jerry and the pimp, but inside he was thinking about the women like Honey and other women who had it even rougher.

It was a matter of control. Pimps and slavers operated the same way. They found the girl's weakness and then exploited it until there was no escape. If a girl had a thing for drugs, they supplied heavier drugs, stepping her up until she was addicted to the pimp's supply. She was his then.

Fear was another tool. If beatings worked, then the girl got thrashed within the edge of her life and that memory kept her in line forever.

Some women were charmed into the life. Others sought it out, looking for glamour and finding dirt. Others were simply grabbed and shipped away and then the techniques were used.

The men around Dartanian were masters at their craft. They knew how to break a girl. The first step was to isolate her from friends and family. Next came the seasoning. A new girl was gang raped and degraded for days on end. They were beaten if they possessed a spark of resistance. After they were seasoned the women were too ashamed to confront anyone in their past. They were no longer independent or human. They were pieces of property.

Pimps bought and sold their girls to one another like ordinary people bought and sold cars. Slavers took it one step further.

The man sitting among them, soaking up the chat and the names that spilled from drunken and coked-up tongues, was about to trace those steps to the top.

After a week of barcrawling with Jerry, Dartanian had him psyched. He knew how to work him and the gang. By Tuesday night he was ready for a breather.

He needed the free time to slip back into his real personality and wash the dye and despair that infected his undercover identity. These people were sick and soon he would give them the cure.

Mick Porter and Sin Simara showed up at the Cage Street headquarters at ten o'clock in the evening. Like other ICE cases, this was a 24-hour deal. It was impossible to separate work from relaxation. Shortly after they arrived, they began talking about their work; it was their life. Just as cops sought out the company of other cops, ICE agents sought men who fought the same fight. ICE ran in their veins.

They relaxed in the apartment next to Dartanian's office and periodically dropped shoptalk to unwind. Dartanian took two beers from the refrigerator and handed one to Mick. He tossed a cold can of celery juice to Simara, who had thoughtfully stocked Dartanian with a year's supply.

Both men stuck to just one beer. More than one wasn't enjoyable; it was dangerous. In their line of work a call to action came at a moment's notice. Too much alcohol dulled the edge, slowed a man's reflexes, and invited a bullet.

Dartanian put an album on the Bang & Olufsen stereo system. *Saturday Night Miles.*

"Do we have to listen to this every time we come here?" Mick said. "Why don't you play something nice? You know, some classical music like *Brazil 66.*"

Simara snickered.

"What now?" Mick said.

"I'm not one to correct a jackass, but you apparently misunderstand what classical means."

"Please. No lectures. And what would you like to hear?"

"*Jade Warrior* would be nice," Simara said.

Dartanian avoided the argument by switching the

selector from phono to an FM station. He preferred to have music in the background. Initially, it was just to jam any mikes that might be around, but over the years he'd come to appreciate music for its own sake. Even in the DSS building which was virtually bug-proof he often played music, especially the early jazz albums of Miles, MJQ, and Dave Brubeck. They seemed to be alive and hopeful, music from a better day.

"How are things in the slave business?" Simara asked, and suddenly there was no music at all. Dartanian's loathing for the gang he had to befriend drowned all sound. He thought for a moment before answering, picturing the ruined women he'd seen, the foppish pimps, and cut-throat slavers.

"I'm in solid with them," Dartanian said. "Especially Jerry. He talks to me a lot about the girls he's had and the girls he's going to get and the money he's going to spend."

"Better spend it while he can," Mick said.

Dartanian nodded. "From what I've picked up so far, it seems Storm is the main buyer for Jerry's women. He deals with others, but mainly Storm. The pipeline goes from Storm to a bigger broker in Montreal—or Storm deals directly with some select customers. I think Cindy went to the Montreal pipeline. The man is Denaud; he's a power hitter. I've got the computer working on it now."

"When do we start?" Simara said.

"It's starting now. I've picked up a lot of names in Jerry's circle. We hit them, leave Jerry's footprints, and start a gangwar. That should give him the push to clear out of town and take care of his other business. He wants to hit Cindy, but he's moving real slow. I want to start him on the way and throw him a curve."

"What kind of curve?" Mick said. "Not that I don't follow or anything."

"Our gal Val," Dartanian said.

Montreal swung at night. Glittering nightclubs, chic cafés, and a hundred theaters beckoned the well-dressed herd that cruised the city after dark.

St. Catherine Street was usually the most active since it was a central thoroughfare in Montreal. The east-west strip covered action from high life to low. The street offered the Place des Arts entertainment complex, the Forum rock and sports arena, and a score of hotels and bars favored by the in-crowd. Anyone with money to burn and hungry for a good time automatically became part of the in-crowd.

Midway between Atwater Avenue and Crescent Street was a place called Les Dames. The otherworldly strip palace was wedged between two porno movie houses. It was Thursday night and Les Dames was packed with regulars. Sprinkled among them were businessmen on a lark and tourists soaking up sin.

Blue lights bathed the stripper on stage. She had large breasts favored by Les Dames customers and her magnificent ass was often featured on promo posters in the alcove. The stripper was an enticing lure for window shoppers who couldn't make up their minds whether or not to step inside.

Her name used to be Cindy Barrington. Now it was Colette, the French sexpot from Paree. *Come inside and experience her*, said the copy on the posters. She didn't know the connection between her presence and increased revenues at Les Dames because it wasn't her business to know such things. It was her business to satisfy the customers. She did that by bumping her hips from left to right beneath skintight leopard panties.

Cindy turned her back to the audience and rested

her hands on her hips. She leaned forward as far as she could stretch. In sync with the heavy bass of the jukebox jazz she jerked her ass up and down until whistles and wolf yells drowned out the music.

With a triumphant smirk, the redhead stood suddenly and turned to the audience so her breasts waved at them. She hooked her thumbs into the taut waistband of the skimpy bottom and then teased the crowd with a reluctant pout.

"Go ahead, darling!" a drunk in a loose fitting suit shouted.

The corner of her mouth twitched like she was about to shout back at her front row admirer. She thought better of it and gave them what they wanted. A murmur spread through the crowd as she went into her skit with the bearskin rug. Every stripper did the same act, but none did it like Cindy. She was fresh and there was a shy quality as she sprawled on the rug. It was childlike and it was box office. She cried and gasped and licked her lips while she pretended that a phantom lover had mounted her.

The cries from the crowd stopped. They were under her spell, staring and drinking and breathing hard. Each man wished that he could take the place of the phantom riding her hips.

It could be done for the right price. The whispered policy at Les Dames was to auction the strippers to the highest bidder. Immediately after her act, customers in the know could bid by simply raising a finger. A hostess stopped at the table to record the bid. The winner was then served a house cognac for which he paid the price of his bid. Then he was entitled to a backstage, backroom visit.

Stripping was no longer an art. It was merely an advertisement of the goods for sale. It was paradise for the customers, hell for the strippers. The client's dreams and the stripper's nightmares crashed together in a bed upstairs.

Cindy finished her act, took her bows, and stared out into the audience. She wondered who had won the sex lottery. For a moment a strange look passed on her face, a pleading gaze that begged the crowd to go home and leave her in one piece. She didn't know if she could take another customer tonight. Cindy was losing her mind as well as her body.

A thousand tears ago she had been a senator's daughter living the good life of the upper class. She escaped that for the bohemian milieu in New York to become her own person with a new name and a new life. Now she was beyond all that. She had been taken to an alien environment with no contact with the outside world except for those monstrous degrading sessions with the customers. Colette was gradually becoming her real and strongest identity. She had to submerge her past if she wanted to have a future.

There were too many obstacles to ever think of escaping or contacting her father. She didn't want him to know what happened. She couldn't face him, and she was afraid to try it anyway. Cindy had seen the punishments of Pierre Denaud and had no desire to feel them.

Her only course of action was to please and obey. Other thoughts were blocked out of her mind by the wanting to go on living. The redhead stripper had been conditioned well. She had become an empty-headed vessel of pleasure.

She waited backstage for her introduction to the highest bidder. She previewed what would happen. First the introduction, then the flesh grabbing, then the trip upstairs. Les Dames had forty rooms on the second floor, some of them equipped to satisfy special tastes. The third floor contained a fully-equipped movie studio and film processing lab. The other floors had small apartments for some of the girls and for the rough boys that lived at Les Dames. Denaud kept a penthouse apartment on the top floor where he occasionally entertained guests, plying them with food, drink, and girls like Cindy. Sometimes he stayed there, sometimes at his townhouse in Old Montreal. And there was his estate in the country. Cindy had been taken to every one like a brand new trophy to be admired and passed around.

After a short rap on the door to her dressing room, Jean stepped inside. He was the black-tie hulk, who helped keep the peace at Les Dames. The drunk who shouted at her from the front row was with him.

"This is Mr. Smith," Jean said.

He mumbled something she couldn't understand and then followed her upstairs to a room with a four poster bed. She gave him a vacuous smile perfected in the dozen X-rated loops she performed in and then she gave him her dream flesh. He kept his tie and shirt on and climbed on top of her. His hands took her breasts while her face sank into the pillow. His tie whispered across her bare back for three minutes until he came.

She hurried him out of the room, washed up, and then went back downstairs. She had another act in forty minutes. Until then she had to work as a hostess. The uniform was basic black with short skirt, stockings, low-cut top, and soft black gloves. It was the cultured whore look.

The minute she entered the bar a chill swept her spine. It wasn't because of the skimpy hostess garb. It was because of the cheerful smile of Pierre Denaud who swooped down on her like a carnivore to a lamb.

"You were quite lovely tonight," he said. He steered

her behind the long bar that ran the full length of Les Dames.

"Yes, Mr. Denaud," she said.

He ran his fingers under her soft chin. "Too lovely to ruin for a minor infraction." His fingers stiffened and poked into her throat. The nail was sharp as it whisked across her neck like a guillotine. Denaud pressed hard until she choked. "Too lovely, eh? Unless you force me to act."

She stayed mute. To do otherwise courted disaster.

"You and Erica have broken the rules. You insult my customers. You talk back and act cold to them. You forget what you are and where you are."

He was very polite. His smile never changed. Pierre Denaud always kept his emotions in check. The handsome face never lost control. He was smooth complexioned even though he'd seen fifty. Gray tinged his short sideburns and streaked his charcoal hair.

Despite common knowledge that he was a killer, narcotics and weapons dealer, and slavemaster, Pierre Denaud fancied himself a man of culture. He always wore evening dress and he always smiled. He could laugh with a girl one minute and slash her face the next.

"Stay down here after we close tonight," he said. "You and Erica. You might learn something."

Cindy nodded her head. Whitefaced and penitent, she bit her lip in fear.

"Smile or I'll cut you where you stand."

She smiled.

It was returned with a flash of brilliant white teeth. "Very nice," Denaud said. "Remember to smile at me in front of our customers, eh?"

"Yes, Mr. Denaud," she said. She smiled, and then went out to mingle with the customers. She took orders for drinks, hands on her thighs, and drunken offers to show her a good time.

Meanwhile Erica did her turn on stage. She had silver hair that shimmered under the blue lighting. Metallic silver cups hid the treasure chest beneath her futuristic costume. Despite her lush figure and her wanton gestures, Erica was awkward and sloppy on stage. She staggered through the music with glazed eyes. But the men didn't notice her eyes and they goaded her on with wolf pack cheers.

Cindy periodically watched Erica perform but she lost herself in taking care of the customers and then doing her own act. She had learned not to dwell on what was coming to her. Once they saw fear they doubled their efforts. To them fear was a bone to a dog.

At the end of the night Pierre Denaud and Louis Eglise came up behind the two women sitting at the bar. Erica was stewed as usual. She thought that Denaud kept her afterhours for a party. She chattered with Cindy and didn't even notice the bartender cut out at a nod from Denaud.

The platinum-haired stripper crossed her legs, drained her whiskey and soda. She toyed with a pearl necklace that dipped into her blouse. Erica was submerged in a stupor. She'd been brutalized for years. Whenever a girl was needed for a rough trick she was picked. She drank at every opportunity.

Erica suddenly realized the men standing behind her hadn't said a word. She stared at their images in the bar mirror and tried to keep cool.

"Hello, Erica," Denaud said. He was smooth as silk with a honeyed voice and a gentle smile.

"Well," Erica said. "We gonna have a party?"

"You are," Denaud said.

Erica looked at Cindy for help. The trapped expression on the platinum stripper's face made Cindy turn away. There was nothing she could do.

Denaud grabbed the necklace, twisted it around his fist, and yanked her head back. Her brightly-dyed straight hair swept over his knuckles.

"Uhhhh!"

"Wait," he said. "It gets better." He tightened the pearl noose. Erica gasped. Her face turned purple until the string broke and the pearls bounced onto the bar.

"What did I do?" she said. "Whatever it is, I'll make it up to you. Let me make it up to you, please, just like in the old days." Her voice rose in pitch as she begged the vicelord.

Denaud shrugged. "See?" he said to Cindy. "See how she runs her mouth?"

Cindy nodded.

Denaud backhanded Erica's face and spun her around on the bar stool. She turned completely around in a circle. It would have been funny if there weren't knuckle marks on her cheek.

"What did I do?"

"You talk too much." He slapped the other cheek and spun her around again. She buried her head in her hands. "Last night you spoke to one of your clients about me. You told him all sorts of horrible lies. Fortunately the client was one of my men."

Cindy wondered what was in store for her. Was Erica just the warmup for him? Were Cindy's supposed sins worse than hers? Denaud had spies, goons, and informers planted throughout his nightclubs and periodically they checked out the girls to see how she treated a customer. Denaud got a full report. He cultivated an aura of paranoia; none of the girls knew who to trust, even among themselves.

"I've heard a lot of strange comments about you,

Erica. You've said too many things to too many people. The only cure is to make sure you say nothing from now on." Denaud nodded to Louis. "Bring them in."

Louis Eglise went down the hall and came back a minute later with four young hoods. They had expensive stomping boots and leather jackets.

"Mr. D, how are ya? It's good to see ya." The gang leader strutted towards Denaud. He had uneven curly black hair and a mangy half beard.

"Fine," Denaud said. "And you?"

"Yeah, I'm fine too. What's the story? It's nice of you to have us down to your place, man. But why? What's going on?"

The three other toughs looked the place over. They were between 18 and 22, the vicious years. Les Dames met their approval. It was plush, the kind of place they'd have if they played their cards right and followed their leader, Philip.

"You gentleman are here because I wish to reward you for your favor last week."

"Oh, you mean the chiseler we busted up for you. We got him good, Mr. D. He won't mess with you no more."

Denaud winced at the mention of the deed. In his world it wasn't proper to be specific. Denaud and his kind always talked around what they did. Victims were referred to as problems. Killers were expeditors, drug dealers were merchants, and slavers were field reps. The worse the crime, the more civilized the tag.

"Yes," Denaud said. "The problem you solved deserves something extra." He grabbed Erica's elbow and hauled her off the stool. "She's all yours." He threw her face first to the floor.

"What's the deal?" Philip said. His three partners looked at Erica with savage delight.

"Take her," Denaud said. "She's on the house." He sat on the stool he'd just thrown the stripper from. "Louis will give you a hand. The lady needs a lesson."

Louis motioned for the leather-jacketed men to follow him. They herded her with shoves and slaps and took her down the hallway.

It took almost a half hour.

During that time Denaud stayed with Cindy at the bar. He didn't say a word to her the whole time. Instead he went over the ledgers with total concentration, as if he'd switched off Cindy until he wanted her again.

Louis escorted a shaken and bruised Erica back to the bar. Her clothes were in tatters. Her lips were bleeding and her eyes were clear. She sat next to Denaud.

"Have we learned our lesson?"

Erica looked numbly at him.

He repeated the question. His voice had a beseeching tone as if the only thing he cared about was her welfare. He shrugged when she didn't answer. "Ah," he said. "Just to make sure . . ." He grabbed the back of her neck and pushed down hard. Erica's face thudded into the smooth mahogany bar. It stayed there.

"Get her out of my sight," Denaud said. "Ship her ass to the sadist in Nice. Give him a discount and my regards, eh?"

Louis dragged the unconscious stripper away.

Denaud and Cindy were alone at the bar. It was the middle of the morning, dark and eerie in the plush bar. "I hope you have learned something," he said to Cindy.

"Yes."

"Good. Perhaps you will share your knowledge with

the other girls, eh? Don't leave anything out. You might become the next Erica."

"I'll tell them," Cindy said.

"Of course you will," Denaud said. "Well, it is late. I'm staying here tonight. All this commotion has me excited. Come to my quarters in ten minutes."

She smiled at the sick bastard. "Ten minutes."

Denaud made a slow dignified exit. Cindy poured a stiff drink.

—————————— *Six* ——————————

White sheer curtains rustled across the windowsill. The silky scratch woke the girl. "Who's there?" she said. "Is someone there?" Her voice echoed in the 3 A.M. stillness. She looked at the billowing curtains that hissed into her bedroom on the warm June breeze.

Absolute quiet terrified her. She clutched the white satin bedsheet and dropped her head silently onto the pillow. Her heartbeat drummed until a floorboard squeaked in the hallway and scared her stiff. The instinctual paralysis passed after 30 seconds but her flesh stayed chilled.

"Who is it?" she said.

Two men froze. They relaxed and breathed low and deep. Like children caught in the statue game they held their pose. Their next move depended on the young woman lying in bed. Her mind would tell her to go back to sleep because everything was fine and she was hearing only the normal sounds of night. Her body would tingle with warnings that her brain didn't want to recognize.

61

Dartanian looked down the hallway of the railroad flat through the dining room, kitchen, and into the target area—Carol Sutherland's bedroom.

Martin stood beside him. It was a special occasion for him. Normally Jerry had all the fun. Jerry charmed the girls, bedded them, and then hauled their pretty drugged asses out to the waiting van. This time the plan had to be changed.

Carol Sutherland was smarter than most. She took time to check Jerry out and discovered there was no such record producer by the name of Jerry Quandt working for RBS Records. By then she'd slept with him a dozen times, dreaming a silly Hollywood romance. Jerry would discover her and make her a star, a sultry torch singer. Carol was hungry for success but not blind. She chopped up his excuses when she confronted him with her discovery.

They had a screaming wall-kicking fight that ended with Carol threatening to call the cops. The pervert was just one more user who would do anything to get her body. She tossed him out on his ass in broad daylight and followed him up the sidewalk, shouting "sick degenerate creep" loudly enough for half the block to hear.

Tonight she would find out just how accurate her opinion of Jerry was.

"Take her or waste her," Jerry had said less than a half hour ago. "She knows what I look like and she's the type to blab it all over town. We can't take a chance on her."

While Jerry fumed in the van about what a queen bitch Carol Sutherland was, his two hitmen stood like stone in the middle of Carol's flat.

Behind them was an open door with three picked locks.

The bedsprings squeaked. Carol's bare feet made a

thumping sound on the wooden floor. She stood in the doorway and peered down the hall. "Is someone there?"

"Now!" Martin said. He ran down the hall. Dartanian was a second behind him. Carol half ran, half fell into the bedroom. She was beyond screaming. The panicked songstress scrambled to her feet and edged away from the door.

Martin slammed the window shut while Dartanian closed the door behind him. Carol jumped onto her bed. The matching satin bedspread and pillows glowed from the slab of moonlight through the window. The entire bedroom was plush and expensive. It was a romantic setting for a girl with dreams. The two nightmares in black didn't belong in the dreams.

Carol sat back on the bedboard. She looked like a brunette in a horror movie facing some hideous monster. She had a showgirl face and body, and fear-parched lips. She wore a long white t-shirt with a silver sequined butterfly below her jutting breasts.

Dartanian felt ashamed at the sight of the petrified girl. But Martin was having a ball. Terror was his favorite pastime.

Carol shivered. Her eyes moved from man to man. Instinctively she stared at Dartanian and shied away from Martin. "What do you want?" she said.

"We're flexible," Martin said. "When I came in here I just wanted one thing, but now that I see you, darling . . ."

"Don't scare me like this," she said. "Please."

"Hey," Martin said. "It's the only way I know how." He looked at Dartanian to see if he shared in the joke but he couldn't tell what was going on in those computer-calm blue eyes.

"I'll scream," Carol said.

"Go ahead," Martin said. "There's no one home

upstairs. And the old coot downstairs is practically deaf. Besides, sweetheart, people don't hear screams anymore. It's not safe."

"How do you know all this?" she said. "Who are you?"

"It's our business to know these things," Martin said. He whipped out his FN Browning Hi-Power and pressed it into her ribs. He moved the barrel until it lifted her left breast.

"Cool it," Dartanian said.

"Hey, man, I'm just having fun." He grabbed Carol and pulled her to her feet. "Turn around. Hands over your head. Spread 'em."

He lifted the t-shirt over her shoulders and frisked her. "She could be packing, you know?" He laughed and looked back at Dartanian, urging him with his eyes to have some laughs. Dartanian was stone faced. Martin shrugged and caressed her back with the Hi-Power. "You're gonna enjoy this, darling," he said. His free hand tugged down his zipper.

"Try it and you get banged, too." Dartanian said. His low and clear voice turned Martin around. He saw the ASP 9mm pistol gripped in Dartanian's hands. It was aimed at Martin's head.

"What's the matter? You can have her too."

"No more fucking around," Dartanian said. "We got a customer to keep happy and he won't accept spoiled goods."

Martin tucked the Browning inside his black jacket and stepped away from the girl. "Do your stuff, hotshot," he said.

Carol sensed they weren't going to kill her. She also picked up on the customer number. She knew she was someone else's goods. Hot goods. She jumped and stamped both feet on the floor. She did it twice before Martin knocked her off her feet.

The heavy breasted brunette landed flat on her back in the middle of the bed. Dartanian pressed a chloroformed handkerchief over her face. It was the oldest technique to knock out a subject, and it was the best.

Carol squirmed and kicked. She tried to breathe through her mouth, but Dartanian stuffed the cloth in her lips. She inhaled. He held the cloth over her nostrils until she went limp.

The girl was smart, he thought. The old man downstairs was hard of hearing but the pounding she gave the floor could jolt him awake.

Dartanian rolled Carol's t-shirt down to make her look like a presentable fun loving drunk. He and Martin took an arm and lifted her from the bed. In the living room Martin flicked a brass floor lamp on and off to alert the van.

They carried her downstairs with no problem. Her slender feet glided softly over the carpeted steps. At the front of the building a door flicked open, spilling light into the hallway.

"Hold it right there." A sixty-year old warhorse confronted them with a 12 gauge shotgun. Carol *had* succeeded in waking him. The gray-haired warrior felt no fear. What he felt was a sudden metal slap on the head.

Martin slammed the barrel of the shotgun into the man's forehead and took a chunk out of his skin. He grunted and fell back into his brightly lit room, sprawled out in front of a ragged easy chair.

The man made two miscalculations. First, he thought the sight of the shotgun would stop any prowler. Second, he misjudged how quickly Martin could close the space between them. He'd been hit even before he had a chance to aim the shotgun.

"Fucking hero," Martin said.

The old man had guts, Dartanian thought. He didn't deserve any pain. He deserved a medal, not the terrible gash from the bridge of his nose to his hairline.

"Let's go," Dartanian said.

"Yeah," Martin said. He thudded his boot into the dangerous man's ribs. That boot was the seal of approval on Martin's death sentence.

They carried Carol Sutherland into the street and tossed her into the van. Jerry pulled her roughly across the carpeted floor. The van took off a second before both doors clicked shut. In half a minute they were a block away.

"This bitch has given me a lot of trouble," Jerry said. "I feel like paying her back something hard." He lifted the t-shirt like he was unveiling a work of art. For a moment he forgot his anger and appreciated the cold unconscious body.

"The customer's a pretty mean dude," Dartanian said. "Cold as ice, man. If he sees we roughed her up the deal's off. Maybe some lead starts to fly."

"Yeah?" Jerry said. "So there is something you're afraid of. This customer of yours must be some tough Chink."

"Japanese," Dartanian said. "Yeah, he's tough." He had engineered this deal with the customer. Jerry had the victim all picked out and ready for delivery to Storm until Dartanian promised twice the price for Carol Sutherland as long as they dealt with his customer.

Money was the language they all understood. Money and kicks. That was why Jerry wanted them both. "Okay," he said, leaning back against the vibrating wall of the van. "So he's tough. That makes it richer. Let's all do a number on the chick, deliver her for the bucks, and if he complains, we waste him. Then we sell her ass to Storm. Dig it?"

Dartanian shook his head. "Try it if you want," he said. "But she's gonna be the most expensive piece of ass you ever had. It could cost you your life."

"Wooooh!" Jerry said. "You're serious, huh. Alright, let's play it out. See what happens when we get there."

It was a typical attitude. Dartanian had seen it in the drug rings, and now in the slave rings. If a crew had a chance to rip off their customer they'd go for it. Along with dealing narcotics they dealt death. If anyone was silly enough to walk into a deal without being armed to the teeth they were begging for a coffin.

That was how these people did business, Dartanian thought. This was their career. Instead of nine to five, it was midnight to six. Their offices were bars and their work was misery. God help anyone who got in the way.

Jerry had the brunette spread out on the platform in the back of the van. He shook his head in regret, patted her on the ass, and then put her out of his mind. He lit up a cigarette and stared at the red glow.

Dartanian lit a Pall Mall and relaxed with his good buddy. The van rocked gently as Stu wound them through Manhattan. From time to time a horn sounded as some drunk took out his frustrations on the empty back streets. By quarter to four in the morning they were out of the city.

"Stu, you got the directions straight?" Dartanian said.

"You gave 'em to me, didn't ya? I got it straight."

Martin sat wordless in the passenger seat. He fiddled with the radio and looked at the Hudson on their left. He pretended no interest when Dartanian went over the details of their hit on Carol, but he listened.

Jerry asked about the delay. "You signalled and

then you came out a year later. Meanwhile we pulled up in front and played with ourselves. What happened?"

"Al Capone there," Dartanian said, nodding towards Martin, "wanted to leave a body there to make things hot." He told Jerry about the old man and how he went down.

"Yeah, well," Jerry said.

"There was no need," Dartanian said. "What he saw was some shadows in a dark hallway. We coulda finessed our way out of there and gave the old man a line. Now we got one wracked-up gent to draw the heat."

"So there'll be heat for a while," Jerry said. "The guy's not dead, right? The cops will waltz around and then call it an unsolved mugging. And the girl? Bam. She took off with a lover." The young slaver unraveled the explanation from experience. "No one will ever put it together."

The man who put it together and was about to tear the whole network apart nodded and smiled.

When they passed through Croton-on-Hudson, a sharper mood came over the men in the van. It was a tense battle atmosphere. In this business nothing was ever taken for granted. They had to be ready for anything.

Just before they reached Montrose, Stu crossed over a set of railroad tracks and eased the van onto the dark edge of the shorefront. He killed the headlights and followed the widening and shrinking strip of sand between the Hudson River and the tracks.

The van's heavy tires sank into the moist debris-strewn beach where a shallow pool had formed. Water sprayed over the windshield as the van lurched hard to the left. Stu corrected the problem by shouting, "Sonofabitch motherfucker!" and steered into the skid. He zigzagged the van until it was out of danger and the Hudson River was a good ten yards to the left. "Nice directions," he said. "Hop the tracks. Kill the lights. Follow the beach until we see the signal. You forgot to say jump in the river."

"Yeah, well," Dartanian said. He was beginning to adopt the language of the gang. Whenever fate intervened and a man had no choice but to accept what was coming he said "Yeah, well", and that was the end of it.

A wide flashlight beam sliced through the night. It came from the railroad tracks. A second beam came from the shore. The beams met and formed a finish line on the sand.

Stu slowed the van to a crawl, made sure he was on firm ground, and then parked at the line. Two shapes dressed in black cloaks held the beams perfectly still.

"Man, they're wearing gook clothes," Stu said. "That stuff gives me the creeps." He stared at the shapes clothed in dark robes from ankle to head. Their feet were bare and white in the moonlight. Shadowed eyes peeked out from the black cowls.

"Same as us," Martin said. "Night gear. Ready for getting it on. But those fellas count on that kung fu crap. I think we can waste them."

"What do you think?" Jerry said. He looked at the men standing on the beach.

"This is just the welcoming committee," Dartanian said. "Take a look out on the river."

Stu and Martin had already noticed the boats drifting alongside a rickety dock. The waters of the Hudson rose above the moorings and just the tide splashed surface of the dock was visible.

Jerry craned his neck forward between the front seats of the van for a better look. "Fucking A," he said.

A black V-planed speedboat bobbed twenty yards offshore. Two men hung assault rifles over the side like fishing poles.

On the other side of the dock was a 30-foot cabin cruiser. It was as black as the cloaks of the men on shore. A man leaped from the bow onto the dock. Then a launching party followed suit.

The sound of running footsteps joined the sloshing of the waves against the dock. A half dozen men formed a gauntlet leading from the dock to the van. The robed men carried Galil assault rifles. The 5.56 mm Israeli weapons fired 650 rounds a minute. The illuminated front sights made them ideal for night sniping. The lead man of the gauntlet had his rifle fitted as a grenade launcher.

"What do you say we charge them?" Dartanian said. "It'll be like taking candy from a gorilla."

A thin shape walked through the gauntlet and stood in front of the van. "Bring out the girl," he said.

Dartanian eased the unconscious Carol Sutherland from the platform. Her warm, tender body weighed pleasantly on his shoulders.

The men in the van took MP40 submachine guns from a compartment built into the floor. The German weapons would put up a good fight with the Galils of the robed men, Dartanian thought. It would be a nice test. Some other time, maybe. He had to pull off the charade.

He knew they were Galil rifles because he just bought twenty of them a week ago. They came from the estate of a 'collector' who died in a SWAPO ambush in Angola.

"Damn, I hate staying in here. We're like sardines waiting for the twistkey," Martin said, chatting down his nerves.

"If anybody comes out besides me and the girl, we're all dead."

"Can't trust anybody these days," Martin said. He focused his attention on the gauntlet in front of the van and calculated how many he could get with his first clip.

The slender man in the black robe approached the van from the side. When Dartanian opened the door and carried the girl out, the man peered into the van. His eyes promised death to every man inside if they tried anything. "He brings the girl on board, you get paid. Anybody follows him . . ." He pointed to the man with the grenade launcher.

Dartanian followed the slender Japanese man through the gauntlet of Ninja-robed man. He paused at the last man, a wide and tall sort. "Look a bit shorter, will you?" Dartanian said. "You're supposed to be Japanese."

Mick Porter's muffled laugh answered him.

Dartanian followed the Asian connection aboard the cabin cruiser. The 30-footer was on loan from the DEA. It was a pleasure yacht that formerly carried bales of marijuana from a smuggler's mother ship to the shore. There was no trace of the bullet holes that wiped out the entire crew.

The V-shaped speedboat was also confiscated goods. It was equipped with radar scanners, infra-red night vision scopes, state of the art underwater weaponry, and it could do 70 miles per hour. The DEA estimated the value of the racer at a quarter of a million dollars.

Both crafts lent an air of authenticity to the sinister slave broker known as Sin Simara, to Dartanian, and as the Asian connection to the men in the van.

Dartanian brought the girl below deck to the sleeping quarters and gently placed her on one of the beds.

"How'd I do?" Simara said.

"You laid it on a bit thick, but they bought it. You're one tough cookie to those boys."

Simara smiled. "Thank you. I've done some acting in my time."

"Oh?" Dartanian said. "That's new to me, and I got you pretty well covered for the past twenty years. Where did you make your debut?"

"Asian theater," Simara said.

Dartanian groaned. He sat on the bed opposite the t-shirted Carol Sutherland.

"How is it on your end?" Simara asked.

"Great," he said. "After tonight I'm bona fide. You give me the money, I spread it around, and they have twice their usual payment. They understand that and if I get them a better price, hell, I'm God to them."

"It's a shame to waste the money," Simara said.

"It's nothing. Twenty grand? By the time this operation is over we are going to strip this racket clean. Use those creeps' bucks to bankroll their execution."

"We could end it now with one grenade."

"I'd like to," Dartanian said. "But I'll get more names if I stick with them. I get a trail right to the senator's daughter. No. I need them alive for awhile."

"Too bad. Their kind breeds too fast. They might spawn another generation by the time they get what's coming."

Dartanian said, "Look, I gotta get back before they start firing. They are one nervous bunch of hard guys. One bastard smashed an old guy during the pick up. Send a man to check on him." Dartanian gave him the Manhattan address. He picked up the plastic wrapped sheafs of twenty-dollar bills Simara had set aside and stuffed them into his jacket pocket.

Simara looked at the brunette girl on the bed. "If nothing else," he said, "those bastards have excellent taste."

Dartanian headed back up to the deck. "Brief her and keep her on ice. Tell her we're cops investigating a slave ring and if she keeps quiet we'll nab them all. Put her in a safe house until it's over."

"She can stay with me if she likes," Simara said. "I will offer her my own home."

"I'm sure you will," Dartanian said. He jumped off the cruiser and walked down the tide dampened dock. From ten feet away he saw the edgy expressions on Stu and Martin's faces. They were ready to haul ass or kick it.

Dartanian climbed into the van. "Let's hit it," he said. "We got money to burn." He tossed a five grand packet to each man. The van pulled back onto the road with three very happy men inside of it. The all American ethic glowed on their faces. Work hard and you get rewarded. Right now they just received a bonus for all the time and effort they put into their underworld careers.

The usual rate for a grab was ten grand, a good enough price for the work involved. Twenty grand was like getting paid overtime for the same amount of effort.

"Nice bit of work," Jerry said. He ran his fingers over the wad of bills.

Stu and Martin chipped in with their compliments. They were on their way to bigger and better things. Damn, if they kept this new man with them, they'd move up the chain faster than they could spend the money.

"Nice gig," Martin said. "Real nice. You know your business, Lex."

My business is putting you out of business, Dartanian thought. "Glad you noticed," he said. "You aint seen nothing yet." It wouldn't be long before he saw nothing at all.

Seven

Six ICE agents gathered at Dartanian's Cage Street headquarters Wednesday night at nine o'clock.

Sharon Wilde knew something was up. The top floor of the glass tower felt like a launching pad. Rockets were going off tonight. The twenty-six year old dispatcher had learned to read faces in her three years with Dartanian's operation. On these men she read action.

Alex Dartanian had it in his eyes. A penetrating look of fire flashed from his blue eyes whenever he was "on". Mick Porter's massive body gave him away. He was tense and on edge, waiting for an ambush to spring on him. Even Sin Simara wasn't completely himself tonight. The slender Japanese charmer usually flirted with her at length. Tonight he offered to take her on a slow boat to China and passed by her desk without waiting for her customary refusal.

Three men she didn't know well accompanied Dartanian. They were loaded for bear. Sharon had seen them before but they weren't the talkative kind.

Sharon Wilde wondered what was going on inside Dartanian's sprawling office. She had all night to wonder. Four times a week she worked from eight o'clock at night to eight o'clock in the morning. That gave her plenty of time to concoct the craziest scenarios. The attractive brown-haired woman knew one thing, however. After meetings like this, the papers were full of sensational stories in the morning. Underworld fatalities went hand in hand with Dartanian's late night business. Sharon had picked up on the secret nature of DSS by osmosis. She absorbed the tensions and victories and felt very much a part of the crusade. She never discussed her ideas about DSS's moonlighting activities to Dartanian, but she thought that he knew how she felt. That man knew what made everybody tick. She was glad that a man like Dartanian was around.

Inside Dartanian's office five men looked at a map projected on a recessed screen in the wall opposite Dartanian's desk. Three Manhattan locations were pinpointed. Dartanian spoke softly, describing the neighborhoods, the number of people at each location, and their strength. All three targets were staffed by plenty of muscle, but the gangs considered themselves invincible. After all, no one had ever moved against them, so what did they have to fear?

Alex pressed the keys on his desktop computer for a closeup on each location. One at a time the gang headquarters were shown from every conceivable angle.

Videotapes of the gangleaders came onscreen. Sick Maddy Glover lightly stepped into his chauffeured Lincoln. Warner Bund walked down Broadway as if he owned it. Loopy Merrill sat in a bar chewing glass. His face appeared to have been sculptured by a meat tenderizer.

"God, he looks just like Mick," Simara said.

The men sitting on the horseshoe shaped sofa laughed at the image of Loopy Adams in front of them. Even Mick. He was used to Simara ribbing him. Sometimes he struck back, other times he just shook his head like Simara was a kid brother who couldn't stay out of trouble. "Remind me to kick your wise ass back to Japan when this is over, huh?"

"Let's get down to business, gentlemen," Dartanian said. "The three men we've just seen run slave gangs in Jerry's territory. Those gangs and Jerry have an uneasy truce. They know each other, occasionally work together, and occasionally slit each other's throats. It's one big happy family."

Dartanian pressed another handful of keys on the console. Dossiers of each man flashed on the screen, followed by photos of their enslaved women. Some of them were beautiful. Some were dead.

The women were found in New York morgues, back alleys in Montreal, and the streets of a dozen African, Asian, and European towns. The death rate for sexual slaves was more than sixty percent. Not many made it out alive or sane.

"These are only the gangs working in the same area as Jerry. There are a dozen more in this city alone, hundreds across the country, and maybe thousands all over the world."

The information came from the ICE computer. Dartanian accessed his central computer to EPIC, NADDIS, and a dozen more electronic intelligence units. EPIC was the massive computer complex in El Paso that fed on DEA, CIA, IRS, NSA, and FBI reports. EPIC originally specialized in amassing smuggling data but the spiraling web of underworld connections caused it to expand. Now EPIC dealt with nationwide and worldwide crimes of every nature.

NADDIS was the DEA's Washington based network. From a narrow focus on drug activity when it was first set up, the agency's computer gradually encompassed every crime in the book.

Dartanian read that book and a hundred others through the ICE computer. Aside from the intelligence and military computers, ICE was linked to a network of police data banks across the U.S. In an instant he could summon a bio on every known criminal in the country. Unlike the regulation-choked public agencies, Dartanian's team acted on that information.

The blond man in the blue pin-striped suit looked more like a corporate chairman than a commando leader as his practiced hand swept over the computer keyboard. The ICE computer assimilated the information from the other agencies and then printed out a state-of-the-art rap sheet for each gang. Resumes of death.

"The size of the gangs ranges from four to twenty, depending on the number of activities they're in. Some members drift in for a couple of jobs and move on. Others like the short hours and high pay and stay on or form their own gangs." Dartanian sighed as he briefed his men.

The gangs he was pinpointing for an assault were just a drop in the bucket. There were approximately three hundred thousand violent felons in the New York area alone. It was a veritable army, a horde of twentieth century barbarians. Though the hoods and the thugs that plagued the streets were outnumbered by the rest of society they ruled the world. They operated freely because society forgot how to fight back.

A new dark age was coming, a return to medieval times when bandit gangs roamed the countryside. The modern bandits were better armed and had no humanity left. Their crimes increasingly grew more chilling and senseless. Rape and murder was so common that the reports moved to the back of the newspapers to serve as fillers between the advertisements.

Someone had to take a stand and turn the tide back, reclaim America, and sit behind a desk and program the extermination of the talking insects that infested the woodwork of society. The Protector took it on his shoulders because he was born for it. If Dartanian didn't start, no one else would.

"As it stands now, these three gangs, and Jerry's gang, are the actual grab teams. They deliver to a man called Bernard Storm in the Catskills. I've got more information on him, but that's for a later date. The chain from Storm goes north to Montreal, where a man named Denaud moves the women from there on. I believe Denaud is our ultimate destination for the Barrington girl, but it's too early to tell. I'm in good with Jerry but I don't want to press him too hard for information. Too many questions and things might change."

The men nodded. Dartanian got up and sat on the front of his desk. He folded his arms and looked at each man. "Okay," he said. "I'll go over it one more time, then I want each team to study the material on their targets, and then we go out there and kick ass."

He paused a minute and pictured the operation in his mind before speaking again. "We hit these gangs hard but leave some of them alive so they can seek revenge. That throws the whole scene into a gangwar—which we shall orchestrate—and I use the war as a reason to probe for more information. Jerry will really open up when the bullets start to fly. Then we chop off the legs of the slave chain and move up to the top bastards. Remember to throw the blame for these hits on Jerry. I want him running scared."

Dartanian backgrounded his men to the fullest. It

provided data for the attack and strengthened their sense of purpose. These men were deadly but moral. ICE was not a blindly ravaging band of killers. ICE was a way of life. It was an ideal they followed, a struggle they shared.

Sin Simara and Mick Porter were already well briefed but they reviewed the material along with the three new men.

Tim Reed was a former SEAL with plenty of experience in Nam harbors. He'd worked with dolphins as part of underwater combat teams, specialized in demolitions, and could pilot anything that floated. He came to DSS by that instinct that guided most of Dartanian's men. They knew there was an outfit that needed them, just as they needed an outfit that focused on the cause they all shared—returning reality to a wounded America. DSS served as the proving ground, tryouts for the major leagues of ICE. That preserved the security of Dartanian's secret organization. No strangers ever walked into the secret ranks. Dartanian had plenty of time to learn about the men and groom a select few from an already elite squad.

Red Casey had worked for the CIA and the Army as an "animal," Company jargon for an agent who did dirty work. He'd been cut loose from the CIA in the mid-seventies when technical intelligence gathering and propaganda received top priorities. The gentlemen agents looked down on "animals" and were glad to see him go. Just because Red Casey waded in and did the job that had to be done didn't earn him the "animal" tag. He was a soldier and he did what a soldier had to do.

Casey was fifty years old and hadn't slowed down since he was a teenager. He was trim and quick, a master of silent combat. He roamed through Cong territory with an ARVN unit and lived in the jungle. He worked as an interrogator. Casey moved quickly from DSS to ICE, adapting to the concrete jungles of America.

The sixth man was an ex-cop named Larry LaSalle. He was thirty-five with long hair grayed from years of action. Larry worked undercover in narcotics and prostitution. One night in a buy at an uptown project he and two other undercovers were found out and shot. His partners died and Larry spent a half year in a hospital with a bullet in his back. The day he got out, he hunted down the three killers who ran free in the streets, bragging about the cops they wasted. Larry executed them with a riot shotgun.

He was kicked off the force in the ensuing investigation and trial, although every policeman and decent citizen in the city sided with him. The papers ridiculed his "self-defense" acquittal for weeks, but then went on to more murders and entertainment coverage. Larry LaSalle became old news.

These were the men chosen for tonight.

Dartanian took a final puff from his filterless Pall Mall. He stubbed it out in a badge shaped ashtray on his desk and said, "Let's get to work."

He caught a glance of himself in a wall mirror on his way out of the office. His blond hair looked a bit dead from all of the dye he'd used lately but it was unavoidable. Tonight a blond man would make the hit on Sick Maddy Glover. Tomorrow a black-haired man would talk things over with Jerry Cornell and try to figure out who did the hit.

Down in the DSS garage in the basement the teams picked out their cars. Dartanian and LaSalle were working together tonight, but they each took a separate vehicle. Dartanian drove a throwaway car. It was a ten-year old untraceable Buick that wasn't coming back. He jacked the Buick down Cage Street, closely followed by Larry LaSalle in a yellow Audi 5000 Turbo.

LaSalle kept going when Dartanian turned onto West 81st Street. He parked the Audi three blocks away from their target.

Dartanian pulled up in front of a seven-story apartment building on 81st. A man crossed in front of the old Buick. He was thirtyish with a white line scar from his right cheek to his neck.

"How's it going?" he said through Dartanian's open window.

"It's on," Dartanian said.

"Right," the man said. "He's got a dozen men up there. No chicks or citizens from what I've seen. I've been watching for two hours."

"Good," Dartanian said.

"You want me to join in?" the man asked.

"No, we got it covered," Dartanian said.

The ICE agent nodded and walked away. Dartanian sat in the car until Larry LaSalle approached.

The two men went up the steps. Both of them were dressed like they were attending a business conference. There was a doorman but he wasn't serious about checking the people who passed by. Ghengis Khan could have passed him as long as he had a tux.

It was a matter of appearances. Since Dartanian and LaSalle acted like they belonged, and didn't expect to be stopped, the doorman didn't insult them by doing so. They obviously knew where they were going. He nodded to Dartanian as he walked by.

Beneath Dartanian's pinstriped jacket an M61 Skorpion was tucked into his left shoulder holster. His vest held four twenty-round clips. The curved magazines were smoothly distributed, two on a side without causing a wrinkle in the battle tailored suit. On the back of his right hip rested the ASP 9mm pistol in a Bianchi concealment holster.

He was ready for a heated conference.

Larry had an Ingram M11 and a Colt .357 Magnum. He'd grown fond of the Colt during his years on the force. Despite it's high visibility and sound, Larry was never without it. It was much a part of his psyche as his street-conditioned instincts.

The two ICE agents strolled casually down the hall and went into the rear stairwell. They climbed up the dusty steps without meeting anyone.

Matthew "Sick Maddy" Glover lived on the fifth floor. There were three apartments up there, two half sized in front and one large pad at the back for Glover.

His dossier was fresh to both ICE agents. He was called "Sick Maddy" because he was a bleeder. One scratch and the red stuff poured out of him. As a result he was squeamish of any activity that might hurt him. The hypochondriac was afraid that a paper cut would cause him to bleed to death.

He controlled a large gang, sometimes running twenty men. Maddy did prostitution as a logical outgrowth of his business and he moved drugs as well as bodies. Maddy had ambitions.

Maddy Glover earned the "Sick" tag twice over. He loved to see blood run as long as it wasn't his own. Sometimes the women grabbed for resale never made it to the auction block because he went overboard having his fun with them. Though there had been charges against him, none of the knife-slashed female corpses were ever proven to be his handiwork.

A family traced their missing 19-year old girl to Maddy Glover through a private detective and showed up at his place. Maddy welcomed them, acted surprised at their claims, and promised to help find the missing girl out of the goodness of his heart. The confused family went back to their home in the Bronx. That same night a "burglar" broke into their house. He killed both parents and a brother on leave from the army.

The detective vanished.

"Sick Maddy" Glover went about his business. To him it was perfectly logical. There were thousands of beautiful women flocking to the big city every week, creating a wonderful marketplace of flesh for those who dared to play the game. As a businessman, Glover simply filled the needs of a regular list of clients. Who would miss a few women? Better yet, who could do anything about it?

Alex Dartanian and Larry LaSalle climbed the last flight of stairs. Dartanian pulled open the heavy door and looked down the hall. It was empty.

Dartanian pointed at the two overhead lights in the hallway. He stood under the one in the shared hallway between the two small apartments. LaSalle climbed onto his shoulders and unscrewed one side of the fixture. He reached into the glass plate and twisted off the light bulbs. They hurried down to the other end of the hall and repeated the procedure in front of Glover's door.

The hallway plunged into darkness. Dartanian didn't want anyone from the other apartments to get a look at him or LaSalle in case they happened to open their doors in the middle of the action. It was a slim chance but there was no need to risk being identified.

Every Wednesday night "Sick Maddy" had some of the boys over to play cards. It was strickly a stag affair to release the tensions of the trade. It wasn't easy planning the hits, selling the women, and silencing anyone who stood in their way.

The stakes were high, with thousands of dollars on the table for every hand. That kind of bread was play money to Maddy's crowd. The slavers had thousands of potential bank accounts parading through the city in high heels. Every pretty woman was a potential victim to be withdrawn from humanity at a moment's notice.

Dartanian and LaSalle stood outside the door and listened to the half-drunk bullshit from within. "Sounds like quite a party," Dartanian said.

"Yeah," LaSalle said. "Shall we kick open the fucking door or would you prefer I knocked and request an invite?" His mixture of politeness and gutter language rolled naturally off his tongue. LaSalle had worked all levels of the drug trade when he was undercover, from high society to back alley. The street language and society jargon collided and mutated into LaSalle's special rap.

"You have more experience busting down doors," Alex said. "You decide."

LaSalle considered it for a moment. "Actually, the ideal method of entry is to shoot the peckerheaded lock off."

"Call it."

The ex-cop ran his hand over the door. "Sonofabitch," he said. "They got a steel door here. That means there's a crossbar on the inside. Police department used to recommend this type to anyone who could afford it. Figures this bastard would go for it."

"Okay," Dartanian said. "We go in the hard way." He stepped to the right of the door and LaSalle moved to the left. The door was impenetrable but not the walls.

"What if we hit Glover?" LaSalle said. "You wanted to leave him alive and kicking so he could retaliate. What happens if we shoot the fucking gentleman?"

"No tears on this end," Dartanian said. "Let's take the bastards." He unholstered the M61 Skorpion and unfolded the wire stock. It was clipped and ready to rock. The blond headman of ICE adjusted his vest flaps so the standby clips were easy to reach. He threaded the Skorpion silencer on the barrel.

Dartanian looked over at Larry LaSalle. The ex-cop had a salt-and-pepper beard and mustache left over from his undercover days. He looked like he belonged in a café debating Gurdjieff with a raven haired poetess—not in a dimmed hallway outside a slave lord's card party with a sub in his hands.

The noise from the men inside increased. Someone told a joke: Someone swore. They were having a hell of a time.

"Fire a foot high and wave it," Dartanian said. "Like this." He demonstrated the technique by gently lifting and lowering the Skorpion. Firing at a one foot level would catch them if they dived to the floor for cover. If not, their legs would get chopped down in a hurry. "Do the second clip waist high." The second volley would take care of anyone who wised up and sought cover a foot off the floor.

"Got it," LaSalle said.

"Then hit it." Dartanian squeezed the trigger. Chunks of wood dropped to the floor. The 7.65mm rounds ate through the thin plasterboard. Dartanian stitched the apartment wall from right to left. The phyyyt-phyyt sound of the silenced Skorpion was drowned out by the screams inside.

LaSalle blasted away on the other side of the door. Both of them were angled towards the door, weaving a terrible crossfire into the apartment.

Dartanian slapped in a second clip and kept up the fire when it came LaSalle's turn to reload. They stood there like construction workers jackhammering into concrete. Instead of cement they were drilling holes into the bones and flesh.

Return fire slammed through the walls. A couple of

men inside managed to catch their wits and blast the walls with heavy pistol shots.

The ICE agents loaded again and kept up the murderous fire. The twenty round clips picked apart the walls and what laid behind them.

Only 45 seconds had passed but they were wartime seconds. Eternity seconds where every man involved in the sudden gunbattle was fully alert or fully wasted.

The steel door opened and a staggering hulk with a big Webley stuck his head into the hall. LaSalle knocked it off with two shots from his Colt .357. Bits and pieces of the former slaver jumped back into the apartment.

Dartanian saw three or four men moving inside by the far wall, aiming pistols at the door. There was no time to plan the next move. Dartanian went on automatic like the Skorpion and let instinct call the shots. He dove head first into the apartment and sprayed the Skorpion from left to right. The rug was matted with fresh blood. There were torn bodies on the floor, hanging off of chairs, and knocked back onto a blood spotted sofa.

The table that Maddy's men had been using was turned on its side for protection. The wooden oblong surface was studded with 7.65mm stings. Alex saw a man crouching behind it with a .38 raised over the edge, firing blind.

The Skorpion was empty.

Dartanian somersaulted forward, landed on his knees, and grabbed the hand clutching the .38. He slammed the wrist down on the edge of the table and drew his ASP 9mm at the same time. The blond ICE leader fired one shot into the very surprised man's brain. Things like this weren't suppose to happen.

Bullets did not come flying into a room out of nowhere, especially if that room was Maddy's. And death did not come to a tough slave crew so swiftly, so easily. Someone was breaking the rules. Maddy's gang was so used to living on the giving side of a gun. Who would dare go against them?

The man who fell behind the table with a leaking hole in his head was only in his mid-twenties, but the bullet was five years overdue. Dartanian recognized the man from his mug shots. He had been Maddy's protege.

Dartanian sensed movement behind him and whipped around just as a slug burned across his left arm. The steel plowed back his skin in a furrow of wasted flesh. Blood poured down the sleeve of his jacket and streamed over his hand. Alex squeezed off another ASP kicker. He got his would-be killer in the chest and kicked him down to Hell.

LaSalle was mixing it up on the other side of the room. His Ingram was on the floor and he was pinned to the wall by two of Maddy's hoods.

Dartanian took one step towards his partner before a corpse came to life and tackled him from behind. He turned his head when he hit the floor and saw a mindless face of hatred looming above him. The man was hairless as a cue ball and just as smart, a shark bent on ripping Dartanian apart. Alex was pinned but he kicked his legs and jerked his head to the right. A skull-crunching fist thudded into the floor beside his ear.

Dartanian kneed the bastard in the hip and slipped away. The Skorpion and the ASP were knocked on the floor, out of sight. He got to his knees and then saw white lights when the bald man toed him under the chin. His teeth snapped together and his head jerked back until his neck wrenched out of place. The leader of ICE was still dazed by the surprise attack when the man tagged him with a solid roundhouse to his left ribs.

The guy was a methodical killer, always moving forward, always punching and kicking, despite the bullet in his stomach. Dartanian had seen this happen before. The man was like a corpse that would not stop. He operated on bullet-shock and hatred and the will to live and kill.

Dartanian was burning and bruised inside when the bald man came at him one more time. It would be the last time, unless Alex got out of the way. The man had a punching knife in his hand. It was only three inches long. The handle fit around the knuckles and the blade rested between the middle and the fourth finger.

Dartanian scrambled to the overturned card table. It was solid oak with clawfoot table legs. He jumped and snapped out his heavy soled foot. The heel cracked into the wood and the leg splintered free. He bent down to pick up the wooden club.

The huge beastlike man aimed a punch straight at Dartanian's throat. He made a split second calculation. If he swung the table leg like a bat his throat would be gutted before the wood made contact. Dartanian cupped the thick end of the leg in his right hand and guided the tapered clawfoot end with his left. Like he was tossing a shovel full of earth, Dartanian jabbed the sculptured paws at the bald man's face.

It connected a moment before the knife punch reached him. There was no power in the thrust anymore. The blade dropped to the floor.

There was no power in the huge man because the table leg smashed up through his mouth and speared into his brain stem. Dartanian stepped across the room and flung his arms forward, casting into a lake of violence. The impaled corpse flew off the table leg and crashed into the men beating the hell out of LaSalle. They tumbled down to the floor in a heap of bodies. Dartanian waded into the flailing limbs and struck killing punches at Larry's attackers.

Dartanian and LaSalle climbed out of the trashed thug heap. All around them the room was full of men who'd finally got what they deserved. A few of them groaned. The rest had already begun rotting.

"The fucking bleeder's in there," Larry said. He pointed to a closed door midway down the hall. "I was going after him when I got clobbered."

Dartanian nodded. He picked up his ASP and Skorpion from the human rubble.

Three minutes had passed. That put them in the danger zone. The first two minutes of any disturbance went unheeded by most people who heard it. They figured it would go away, and besides, the trouble was happening to someone else. During the third minute they started to worry and considered calling the cops. Any time after that was up for grabs. Anything could happen.

Patrol cops in the neighborhood could show up. Security for the building might show their faces. And it was always possible that one of the tenants might panic and start firing at anything that moved.

"Come on," Dartanian said. He ran down the hall and kicked the door off the hinges with one swift heel. The adrenalin carried him forward into the room. There was "Sick Maddy" Glover cringing in the corner of his bedroom. He had a knife in his hand. It had a jewelled handle and three-edged blade. The weapon was for show, probably used on those unfortunate women who caught his eye. The pale, weak-chinned man wore a bright red shirt with wide lapels, unbuttoned to show off a gold medallion. His hand shook as he positioned the knife in front of him.

"Back off," he said through chattering teeth.

"Kill the motherfucker," LaSalle said.

Dartanian crossed the room. He deflected Glover's knife thrust, grabbed the wrist and twisted it high over his head. He slammed Glover against the closet door and knuckle punched his exposed ribs. Glover folded and choked but clung to the knife, thinking it his last chance to live. Dartanian snapped his shin into his breastbone. The jolt took away Glover's last bit of resistance. The knife fell to the floor and Glover collapsed.

"Listen to me," Dartanian said.

Glover looked up at him from his Buddha crouch and nodded his head. He wasn't breathing well.

"From now on Jerry Cornell gets a cut of your action. He's moving up and out. Go with him or go down." Dartanian pointed the ASP 9mm at "Sick Maddy" Glover.

"Yeah," Maddy said. "Yeah, yeah, no problem." His head nodded like it was on springs. Alex could see that the man had no intention of paying anything. He was relieved that he wasn't going to die. Now that he knew who called the hit, he would land on him with every gun that money could buy.

"You're a smart businessman, Sicko," Dartanian said. "Jerry will get in touch with you to work out the details. For now we'll just take the proceeds from your game."

"Right," Maddy said. He climbed to his feet and sat down on his triple-wide bed. It was positioned in the exact center of the mirrored bedroom. He looked like a dwarf on the bed.

"I'd prefer to waste the prick, if it's alright with you." LaSalle said. He was serious.

Dartanian shook his head. There would be plenty of time for that later. First he would let Maddy plunge the slave network into a gang war. Then Dartanian would come back and pick up the loose pieces. "Let's go," he said to Larry. He glanced at Glover. "Pleasure doing business to you."

They scooped up the unbloodied bills left over from the card game in the other room. The slave money would finance part of Dartanian's war. Only fair to make the slugs pay for their extermination. He looked around the battlefield that used to be Glover's luxurious apartment. It was stained with the blood of Maddy's crew and somehow it looked just right. "Court's adjourned," Dartanian said.

They hoofed it down the stairwell. The apartment building was coming alive with lots of worried voices but no one looked out to see what happened. They wanted to stay alive.

The lobby was deserted. The doorman was nowhere in sight. They hopped into the Buick and screeched down the street. If anyone saw the getaway the cops would get a description of the ratty old car. Dartanian wheeled it the three blocks to the site of the Audi 5000. LaSalle slid behind the wheel of the Audi and punched it down the street while Dartanian slammed the door shut on the passenger side.

Dartanian left the Buick running.

He gave it ten minutes before someone boosted the car and unknowingly led the cops on a wild goose chase. He pictured some poor bastard explaining himself to a detective, wondering just what the hell all this talk about a hit team was.

Eight

Werner Bund was an assumed name. Born as Billy Warner forty years ago in Hell's Kitchen, he had changed his name and his luck when he moved into the pimp business at age 30. The new Werner Bund spoke with a German accent subject to change, sometimes thick and gutteral. At other times it was mellow and cultured, depending on his mood.

The accent attracted women who wanted to move up in life. Mostly they were actresses or dancers who would like to work for Werner. After all, everyone *knew* that he owned several nightclubs in Paris, Hamburg, and Vienna.

Rumors did wonders for his pocketbook. Werner's only connection to clubs in those cities was the women who ended up there as slaves in the eros centers and bordellos. He had no control over their destination. Whoever bought them used them as they wanted.

The gullible fame seekers never realized the truth about Werner's real business until it was too late. He eased them into prostitution by convincing them that a lot of stars began careers that way—until their big break came. He dangled success in front of them like a carrot, and ultimately choked them with it.

If the women couldn't be tricked into sex for pay they were forced into it. The ones who complained too loudly or talked to the wrong people were quickly sold to the highest bidder. In the meantime, Werner's well paid soldiers kept the ladies in line until they made the big trip.

The square-shouldered imposter worked out of the Parisian Hotel on Lexington Avenue. It was advertised on tv as "the place to relax and rediscover the pleasures in life". The clientele in the tv commercials dressed in Bill Blass suits and Dior gowns.

In real life the clientele of the Parisian Hotel was mainly hookers and Johns who rented rooms by the trick. Occasionally a straight tourist couple booked a room and had their minds blown.

Werner owned a controlling interest in the hotel. He lived on the third floor in a suite decorated by equal parts of "House Beautiful" and "Hustler" magazine. It was reachable only by private elevator and special appointment.

Bund periodically held court in the Royalty Room bar downstairs with the other dukes and counts of the night,. He was there Wednesday night when two strangers in black tuxedos caught his eye. They sat at a corner booth and fended off whores. Their drinks piled up untouched on the table in front of them.

Three women in deep-dip summer dresses chattered at Werner, who sat in his regular booth with two of his soldiers. The booths on either side were filled with more of his women under the watchful eyes of subordinates who rented them out. Despite the tough crowd around him he didn't feel safe.

Werner's gaze shifted when the bigger of the two

men looked his way. It was a slow measuring look. Werner felt the eyes upon him, and when he looked back again, the man didn't look away.

The man lit a cigarette and snuffed out the match between his thumb and forefinger. He stared at Werner like he was sending a message.

Werner shuddered. He thought either he was paranoid or else his past was catching up with him. He had a religious upbringing. As a boy it had been drilled into his skull that sins were always punished accordingly. He had found out that wasn't so when he drifted into the underworld. He never got caught, and nothing ever happened to him, but sometimes at night he had dreams about the women he'd ruined, the lives he'd taken. He never could shake off the guilt, and inside the slick Germanic pimp was a little boy looking over his shoulder for a thunderbolt from heaven.

The thunderbolt wore a tux.

Werner had a reputation as a quick man with his fists. Once he'd beaten a man to death in a bar fight. The man was drunk and Werner had help from his men, but he was used to the necessary violence of his profession. Despite his background, Werner felt uneasy. Instinct told him to take a walk.

He got up from his booth and took three men with him. One of the girls who clung to him all night tried to follow. "Not now, sugar," he said. "Stay here until I send for you. We have some things to talk about." The German accent was barely present. Fear peeled it away.

Three seconds after Werner and his crew left the bar, Mick Porter and Red Casey got up from their booth and followed. They moved like athletes performing a well-rehearsed maneuver. They caught up to the men in a short narrow hall that led to Werner's private elevator.

One man looked over his shoulder and gave Mick a warning. "This is private," he said. "Public elevators are over there." He nodded in the direction of the main lobby.

"Right," Mick said.

"So use it." The man had a brutish head with a lot of big teeth showing. He was used to being obeyed.

Mick punched the man's head back in place and followed it with a roundhouse kick to the gut that slammed him against the wall. He grabbed his neck and tossed him into Werner.

Red Casey struck at the same time. He charged into the other two men and bunched them up in the thin hall. His hands and feet slashed out a dozen times while they tried for their guns.

The elevator opened and Werner dived inside. Mick and Casey herded the others into the elevator. They weren't lightweights. They just weren't any match for the ICE agents.

Mick and Casey backed them against the rear of the elevator. Mick trained his .38 Super Auto Colt Commander on Werner, who had the fear of God on his paled face, and the brute next to him. The other two were spellbound by Casey's .357 Ruger Magnum. They gave up their guns one by one. Casey bundled the hardware into one of their jackets and kicked it into the corner.

"What the fuck is going on?" Werner said.

"Stupid, aren't you?" Mick said. The elevator door closed behind him and the car hummed up the shaft.

"Who sent you?" Werner said. "Look, I got a dozen guys downstairs that'll tear you apart, so don't try anything.

"Those guys anything like these guys?" Mick said.

He nodded at the three silent men against the wall. He read their eyes and saw that they were waiting for an opening and were pretty sure that it would come.

Werner had a second-in-command. The ICE dossier was still fresh in Mick's mind with the details on Clark Bruce, a loyal but ambitious man who would fill in the void. Clark wasn't in the bar, and these men all showed signs of hope.

"Anything I should know about your pad?" Mick said.

Werner shook his head.

"How about it?" Mick said to the sweating, fist-bruised man next to the pimp. "Anybody waiting up there? Any special signals we should know about?"

The man shook his head.

"You get a bullet if you're lying to me," Mick said. "Hell, you might get it anyway." He drew a bead on the man's forehead. The man looked at Werner, then at Mick. "Yeah, yeah. There's a code you got to tap."

Mick motioned him forward. He opened a panel above the elevator buttons that revealed a six digit keyboard. He tapped out three numbers.

"Hope it's right, pal."

"It is. That's the "all clear" signal. He won't be expecting trouble."

Werner glared at his man.

"What the fuck do you want me to do?" he said. Clearly, this man wasn't going down with Bund if he could help it.

The elevator opened into a small rectangular hallway. When the men stepped out, Mick hit the talker over the head with the back of his gun hand. He propped him halfway out of the elevator. The rubber-edged door slid up against him. The escape car would be there when they came back out.

Werner unlocked the door to his suite. A moment

later Clark Bruce walked into the room. He was about to say something to Werner when he saw Mick's Colt Commander.

"Over there," Mick said.

Clark joined Werner's two guns and sat down on a modular zebra-striped sofa. Werner stood in the center of the lavishly furnished room.

"Tell me what this is about," Werner said.

"It's about money," Mick said. He talked with his hand, waving the Colt persuasively. "You've been cutting into Cornell's racket, hurting his business. So I'm here to collect what you cost him."

"Cornell? He's small time!"

"What's that make you?" Mick said.

"You sonofabitch, you wouldn't talk like that if you didn't have the gun."

Mick said "Oh?" and dropped the Colt to the chair behind him. Casey stepped back a few feet to cover the sitting men an ample distance away.

Werner held back his smile. He'd been an amateur boxer before drifting into backstreet arenas where he faced other brawlers for money. He thought back to when he killed that man in the bar. He could have wasted the big ox even if he didn't have help from his buddies.

It would be the same with this one.

Werner wouldn't be taken by surprise this time, not like in the hall below. No, this time he would surprise the hell out of this big bastard.

He stepped closer.

Mick dropped his right hand to his thigh. He bent the elbow of his left arm in front of him in the Shorin Ryu style of hard karate that Sin Simara had taught him.

Werner lunged forward with a left jab and a right

hook. Neither of them struck. Instead they were blocked by the brick forearms and wrists of Mick Porter.

The pimp stepped back and then launched a second attack. His speed worked this time. Werner landed a flurry of blows to the body and an uppercut to the chin. Mick didn't strike back.

Werner started to worry. So far his opponent only blocked. He hadn't struck back. He had a premonition that the man was taking Werner's measure and calmly plotting his destruction. Werner saw that in the heartless eyes that never looked away from his own.

Werner saw that Mick Porter didn't regard him as a human being, but as a poisonous insect that had to be exterminated. This unsettling feeling broke Werner's concentration. His attacks went further off target but there was no way he could lose control over the men who served him.

Werner's fists had killed men in the past. They had even killed women, but that was something he kept secret. The fists that made his reputation had no effect on the big tuxedoed intruder.

Werner summoned up the rage created by this stranger, tearing apart his empire, and poured it into a final attack. He gave it his best and whirled into his opponent with eye-gouging strikes.

Mick let down his guard. Werner smiled. He had him on the run. He took the yielded space and moved inside for the kill. He landed a hard punch to the throat and one to the teeth. And then he saw that the dropped guard was bait. It was too late to retreat. He saw the finishing technique coming but couldn't step away.

Mick's arms had been down to his sides, but only until Werner committed himself. Then, like an eagle flying, Mick's arms swooped backwards and upwards in a half circle. The huge fists closed in a pinching blur that landed on the sides of Werner's head at the same time. The side punches crunched Werner's skull and sent bony shards into his brain. Werner Bund went down in a grotesque heap.

"Anybody else?" Mick said.

The men on the sofa stared at the body on the floor. No one met Mick's eyes. "Alright," he said. "Get me the money."

"What money?" Clark said.

"All of it," Mick said. "Every dollar in the place." He picked up his Colt and followed Jerry into a cozy office where he opened a wall safe.

"We can't operate without the bucks," Clark said. "How about leaving a share?"

"It's not my decision. Jerry Cornell said take it all so I'm taking it. You want it back, talk to him."

Clark Bruce was miserable and ecstatic at the same time. He moved up to the top of Werner's operation. But he'd been hit at the same instant. Half of their bankroll was in the safe. He would have to get it back the hard way. He wasn't about to split any of their racket with Cornell. As far as he knew Cornell was small time, and even if he did hire some top muscle . . . Clark Bruce was not about to back down from a war.

Pride was involved. So was greed.

Mick saw the gears working. For now the new boss would play at being cooperative and talk about a meeting with Cornell to work things out. But the minute Mick and Casey left, he would start the war machinery.

Just like the ICE computer predicted.

Casey tied the two men on the couch and gagged them. Mick picked up the money that was going straight to the ICE coffers to help finance the campaign against the remaining slavers.

"Walk us down to the street, will you, Clark?" Mick said. "Just to make sure there's no trouble."

"I'd be glad to," Clark said.

"I kinda thought you would."

As they headed towards the elevator, Mick felt a tinge of sorrow about what had happened in the suite. But it had to be done. If people continued to look the other way, scum would rule the world. It wasn't easy, but it was the right thing to do. The walls of society were crumbling. Somebody had to rebuild them.

The Steeger Avenue home of Loopy Merrill was expensively laid out. The front of the White House colonial gave passersby the impression that maybe a judge lived here, or perhaps a blueblooded banker. It was elegant and well kept by a team of stocky handymen.

This was one case where you couldn't judge a crook by his cover. The only blueblood Loopy ever had was the kind on his hands when he mugged well-dressed older gents who thought Central Park was charming for after dinner walks.

That was when he was fifteen.

He grew bigger and moved on to more profitable crimes, finally earning enough to build the house on Steeger Avenue. Loopy Merrill worked the slavery game. He was crude, ugly, and straightforward, a caveman born a million years too late.

He had a large forehead and thick eyebrows with the furtive look of a man who had been punched one too many times in the head. The shadow brained thug took what he wanted. God help the man, woman, or child that stood in his way.

Since women sold well and they were fun to play with, Loopy Merrill muscled his way into the racket. He killed the leader of the first gang he worked for, took over, and from then on did a high volume business selling women. His assistants stayed on because he paid well, although there was always a risk working for Loopy.

Loopy lost his temper from time to time. Some of his former assistants were in the morgue and some crippled for life, because they had made Loopy angry. Those who still worked for Loopy learned from experience and never complained when he put them to work on the house. They loved to keep up the white colonial.

Loopy's simple mind reduced life to the basics. He slept, ate, robbed, killed, and sold women. He was Idi Amin without brains.

His operation was always spur of the moment. If a prostitute turned him on, he grabbed her from the streets, ran her for a while, and then sold her. Every now and then he picked up a runaway girl at the bus terminal. He picked them out of their nervous line-up and promised to take care of them. Before a girl knew what happened she was out on the streets, pulled along by the ox-like man. The smart ones screamed and ran away, but there were plenty of others who went along like lambs to the slaughter.

Loopy tired quickly of the same girl. He kept her around the house for a while and then if he couldn't sell her ass for keeps—a lot of buyers were hesitant to deal with Loopy—he trashed the girl. His men got rid of the body.

It was a good life.

On Wednesday night a man came to take that life away. Loopy Merrill woke in his darkened bedroom to see a thin man sitting in his Henry VI chair across from the bed. He thought it was a dream at first. Loopy always went to bed at ten o'clock and no one ever disturbed his sleep, especially a tiny little man like this. Loopy blinked his eyes, looked at the man, and snapped his head straight up. The dream didn't go away.

"That's right, Sleeping Beauty. You have company." Sin Simara leaned forward on the chair. He steepled his fingers beneath his chin and stared like he'd just witnessed an extinct species come back to life.

"How'd you get in here?"

Simara smiled. "Your guards out there, Huey, Dewey, and Louie, let me and my partner in."

"They're not supposed to do that."

"They're unconscious at the moment if that makes you feel better," Simara said. "Should they wake they'll be looked after." Tim Reed was out there with a machine pistol trained on the knocked-out men. Aside from the guards on the lower level of the colonial, Simara and Reed had tied up two maids and two hoods in a second floor bedroom. They'd been caught with their pants down.

"Those fucking guys are better than that," Loopy said. He inched up into a sitting position on the bed, revealing a grimy gut stretched t-shirt and boxer shorts.

"They didn't know what hit them," Simara said. "I thought I'd give you a chance to see what hit you."

"Don't make me laugh. What the hell kind of weapon you got, little gook?"

"My body."

"That's what I thought." Loopy Merrill whipped out a gun from under his pillow. He aimed the Colt .45 at Simara who didn't move a muscle.

Loopy pulled the trigger. It clicked. He pulled it six times and dropped the gun on his bed.

"Looking for these?" Simara said, as he flung the steel jacketed bullets at the huge ogre. The bullets stung him and made him roar like a wounded bear. Simara felt him get ready to charge.

Loopy swung his feet over the side of the bed and pretended to be very calm. "What are you doing here?" he said.

"It's time to pay your dues."

"Oh, it's money you want, huh?"

Simara shrugged. There was no reason to talk. Loopy wouldn't understand that Simara was the yin to his yang, lightness to darkness. Besides, Loopy was forming a brilliant plan. He was going to get up from the bed and pound the hell out of the little man.

Chiseled biceps peaked on Loopy's arms when he scrambled from the bed. Ten ways of killing the mountainous scum passed through Simara's mind, but then Loopy decided his own fate. The dull-eyed hulk reached out both arms to strangle Simara. It was a standard move for Loopy that must have worked well in the past. He thundered across the floor.

Simara slapped away both hands with a left-palm, heel block. The big meaty hands thudded into the wall and Loopy cried out. Simara's right hand clenched the huge man's ear and ripped it almost all the way off. The move knocked Loopy head-first into the wall. Simara spun around in a half circle and cracked his elbow into the man's spine.

Loopy slid down to his knees and fell backward, surprise and pain registering on his face. Simara snapped out the heel of his right foot and finished off the beast before he hit the floor.

The carcass spread out on the floor with a caved-in head. It was an obscene trophy, like some wild animal dragged out of the jungle to be stuffed and mounted above a fireplace. Simara could almost hear the ghosts of several slain women singing his praise.

Alex Dartanian had the shadow of a beard on his chin and his face was smeared with sweat and grime from the encounter on 81st Street. He was still in the battle mode, still switched on when he entered his command post on Cage Street.

Sharon Wilde couldn't take her eyes off him. There was blood on his left palm, and he looked like he had just walked through hell. But the blonde man had an aura of energy about him and that aura enveloped the brown-haired dispatcher as he approached.

"Any calls out of the ordinary?" Dartanian said.

"Yes. Mick Porter and Sin Simara called. They each said to tell you 'affirmative' and hung up."

Dartanian relaxed. ICE had come through all the way. There were no major casualties. He walked past Sharon and noticed the way she was looking at him. He smiled at her and stepped inside of his office.

The adjoining apartment was the closest thing to home that Dartanian had. It was as much a part of him as he was a part of ICE. He had a place on Central Park West but that was out of the question tonight. He could not punch out and go home to an apartment to watch tv and get rid himself of the tensions of the day. For one thing, the tensions in his line of work did not fade easily. He was supercharged with adrenalin even though he'd taken his share of punishment tonight.

For another thing, ICE was a 24-hour-a-day business. When Dartanian was on a case he had to be at the heart of the matter. Anything could happen and he had to be ready to respond immediately. The Protector was on call until the campaign was over.

Alex stripped to the waist and looked at the damage. Thin trickles of blood ran from the meaty part of his forearm down to the heel of his palm. The bullet had taken away a four-inch furrow of flesh. The wound was raw and wet. His ribs felt shattered. Every time he breathed a hundred spears stuck at him from the inside.

The damage was nothing compared to the justice he administered tonight. All he had was one more scar to add to the healed white lines that crisscrossed his muscular, sharply defined chest. The dozen or so scars were a roadmap of his past and a hint of his future.

Dartanian leaned over the bathroom sink and rinsed the blood from his arm. He saw movement at the edge of his vision.

Sharon Wilde stepped towards him with a glass of whiskey in her hand. She was nervous but it had nothing to do with timidness. It was excitement that gave her cheeks that flushed look that Dartanian found so appealing. She set the whiskey on the marble sinktop. "I thought you could use a drink."

"You didn't come in here to give me a drink," Dartanian said. He noticed that her white muslin blouse had one more open button than a few minutes ago.

This had happened once before when Dartanian had come back from a late night Icing.

Dartanian took her in a hard embrace. Her breasts crushed softly against his bare chest and then he lifted them out of the tissue thin blouse. They were cream colored and untanned.

There was nothing gentle about their motions. He drew her hips to his and lifted her tan skirt. Seconds later he lifted her bared hips and entered her. She purred and ohhed and hung onto his shoulders.

It was a mutual act with no promises, just desire, and it was quick and good.

Her ass rocked up and down in his hands while her thighs locked around his hips. Sharon bit into his shoulder, gasped, and went limp. Dartanian pulled down on her fleshy hips and followed her orgasm with a series of blasts that drained him from the toes up.

They caught their breath and stepped into the shower. The warm water stung his arm but washed away the meanness of the night. He scrubbed Sharon's back. It was nice. "We'll have to make this short," Dartanian said. "The switchboard."

"Mmmmn-ummmnm" Sharon said. She leaned against the tile with both hands while Dartanian massaged her lathered shoulders. "The next call-in won't be for another forty minutes. And I set the board to transfer any emergency calls to your phone."

"Pretty sure of yourself," Dartanian said.

"No," she said. "I'm pretty sure of you." She turned to face him.

"Thorough, too," Dartanian said.

"Very," she said, and began to prove it.

Nine

The stolen Honda Civic bugged in and out of the sea of cars that poured through Manhattan. It was three o'clock in the afternoon and the Honda felt like a pressure cooker, heated by the June sun directly overhead.

Jerry Cornell didn't look like his usual self as he sat behind the wheel. It was the first time Dartanian had ever seen him unshaven. Instead of nice threads, Jerry wore faded jeans and a dark t-shirt. His sideburns were too long and though he still had good looks about him, Dartanian didn't see how any potential victims could fall for the man. He wasn't together at all. The modern Romeo hadn't slept too well.

"Tell me more," Dartanian said. "I don't see anything to get excited about so far."

"Nothing to get excited about? Are you crazy? I got three fucking gangs breathing down my neck and it's nothing to get excited about."

Dartanian shrugged and tapped a Pall Mall from his pack.

The Honda cut in and out of traffic on the next block. They were on Lower Broadway and at times Jerry went five miles an hour, with forty mile an hour bursts whenever he saw an opening.

"Someone is trying to set me up. Making the hits and dropping my name. I don't believe it." Jerry smacked his hands on the steering wheel. "Some bastard's playing dirty."

The bastard in question nodded his head in sympathy. But inside he was smiling. The hits had done their job. Jerry got a few calls from his friends checking it out and giving him a warning. And then when he made the rounds of the bars where he did business he got a lot of stiff looks from the guys who usually gladhanded him. No one wanted to sit next to him, thinking that any minute Jerry was going to be hit—or that any minute Jerry would waste somebody else.

Word was out that Jerry was poison.

"Any ideas?" Jerry said.

Dartanian leaned back into the passenger seat. His eyes fixed off into space like he was taking a moment to think up a plan. "I got an idea," he said. "But you won't like it. It's not your cup of tea."

"Shoot," Jerry said.

"Right," Dartanian said.

"Come on. Tell me."

"You just said it. We shoot our way out of this. Whether you pulled the hits or not is beside the question. The important thing is that the gangs think you did. We got a war brewing, Jerry. We gotta hit them first. All of them."

"I don't know," Jerry said. "You're right. It's not my thing. Once a war starts it just gets bigger and bigger and we all lose out."

That's the idea, Dartanian thought. "Let's talk about it over a few drinks," he said.

Jerry nodded. He needed something to calm him down. The way he stomped the gas petal every chance he got showed that he was running spooked. Dartanian directed him to a waterfront bar near Hudson Street. It was frequented by dock workers and a few hustlers, but they came to drink and stayed out of one another's business.

They parked the Honda a block away in case the police were looking for it. Dartanian was relieved to step out. He disliked the tin boxes the more he experienced them. The phony gas shortage was calling for smaller and smaller cars. Soon they would all be riding around a mechanized suit of armor on wheels.

In the back of the dark bar Dartanian ordered a couple of beers and whiskey. "You need something to clear out the cobwebs, man," he said.

Jerry nodded. He sipped the beer and sat back into the scarred wooden booth. The eyes that fell on Dartanian were looking for help. "I don't know," Jerry said. "Maybe I can talk things over with some of these guys."

"Forget it," Dartanian said. "You've probably got a price tag on your head. No one's gonna stop and listen when a bullet can make them rich."

"I knew I could count on you to cheer me up."

"Just laying it on the line," Dartanian said. He nursed his beer and ordered another for Jerry. Drink was a temporary retreat for the young slaver. It calmed him down, confused his thinking, and loosened his tongue.

Dartanian probed occasionally, but the crisis that threatened to overwhelm Jerry made him rattle off his troubles while Dartanian sat there calmly. Jerry drank his beer and whiskey. Dartanian drank the names that Jerry spilled.

Jerry Cornell would never talk like this to his other acquaintances, and never in a million years would he breathe a word of his actions to the cops, but to the man sitting across from him in the booth, he told everything.

Dartanian picked through the information and steered Cornell back to any areas that needed clarification. Then he hit him with the gameplan.

"You got to get yourself back together," Dartanian said. "Too many things are digging at you, and if we're gonna solve the problems—I'm not deserting you, remember—you have to let me call the shots."

Jerry nodded. Any other man would have walked out on him the minute trouble started, but this man was staying in the thick of it, ready to haul him out. "Hell, yeah," Jerry said. "You run the show, man." It seemed best to dump it into the hands of the man who could get them out alive.

"Good," Dartanian said. "Have another drink, you make me nervous."

Jerry laughed. He ordered another whiskey to slow down his jumpiness. His fingers tapped on the table and his feet drummed on the dusty floor. He was eager to get on with the business of saving his ass.

"Here's the way it is," Dartanian said. "You have at least three gangs coming for your head, maybe more. And you have some problems with one of your girls. You mentioned it before but you never spelled it out."

"Huh?"

"Some girl named Cindy. You been wanting to track her down. Now's the time to do it."

"Yeah," he said. "Cindy. Damn, you won't believe me when I tell you about Cindy."

"Try me."

Jerry confided what had happened. He talked about the girl he nabbed and sold and how the old Doc messed things up by pulling a ransom stunt that failed. "So now I think I got some Feds after me. Doc really stirred things up. I mean I got a feeling that something is coming my way, something heavy you know. Don't worry, they can't be too close. I'd know, believe me I'd know if somebody was breathing down my neck. Instinct, you know?"

"Right," Dartanian said. "Go with those instincts. They never lie."

Jerry drained another mug of beer. "Yeah, well, it's like this. I nabbed this chick, she was real green, too good to be true. Turns out she had a phony name and she's some bigwig's daughter. A senator no less. She talked once, and she's bound to talk again. Maybe she already has. So I want to seal her mouth for good before this thing comes back to me."

"Okay," Dartanian said. "We make another grab, get some funds, and track down your girl. See, it all works out. We split town for a while, let the gangs hop all over each other, snuff the girl, come back and snuff the bastards that are gunning for you."

Jerry liked the plan. He had gone from a hunted animal to a man on top. Of course he was only on top because he was standing on Dartanian's shoulders, but he didn't mind. He was going to come out of this thing alive.

"One thing," Dartanian said. "Do the other guys know anything about Cindy and the grief she's causing you?"

"You kidding? Stu and Martin can't see past their nose, man. They don't pay attention to shit, man. Money and women and whatever is in front of their eyes at the moment is all they know."

"Good. They'll be easy to maneuver. Now, give me some more on the chick."

"Her real name's Cindy Barrington."

"Barrington?" Dartanian said. "That sounds familiar."

"It should. The girl's father is on tv all the time, you know, Senator Barrington, the guy always calling for defense bucks, a real hawk. He's probably got a damn army looking for me. Coming to save his little girl."

"Probably something like that," Dartanian agreed. He thought back to his most recent conversation with Senator Barrington. The man was in a rough shape. Ready to crack. All because of this bastard sitting across from him.

They stayed in the waterfront bar for another hour. Jerry stepped out of the bar with a head full of alcohol. The hot sun battered his eyes and dried out his body some more.

Dartanian drove the Honda away from the waterfront. Jerry rolled the window down and leaned back in his seat to catch the breeze on his face.

"What about the next grab?" Jerry said. "I don't have anybody in mind. It'll take too long to work on a chick."

"I'll set it up," Dartanian said. "I'll get the chick and you work it out with Storm."

"Fuck, yes," Jerry said. "Let's do it." Drunk and confident, Jerry smiled. He turned on the radio and drummed his fingers on the dash like he didn't have a worry in the world.

Dartanian dropped him at his place off Houston Street. "Anybody know where you live?" Dartanian said.

Jerry hung his head back inside the open window of the Honda. "Nah. Nobody I can't trust, anyway."

"No such person," Dartanian said. "Watch your ass

and think about crashing somewhere else for the next few days."

"Yeah," Jerry said. "I'll think about it."

"Good. Now set a meeting for the guys tomorrow morning. We gotta set this thing in motion." Dartanian drove off. Jerry waved to him, all smiles and drunken brotherhood. Alex dropped the mask of friendship the moment he was out of sight. That man back there had sold Senator Barrington's daughter into slavery. He'd been able to do it because he was a charmer, and because the climate of the country allowed anything to happen. With no punishment from the laws, what kept guys like Jerry from trying their luck at anything that turned up a buck? Nothing. The worst he could expect was a stay in one of the prison warehouses where he'd serve his time and then come out and start over again.

Not this time, Dartanian thought.

He ditched the car in midtown and walked to the Cage Street headquarters. On the way he reviewed all of the information Jerry gave him and committed the names to memory. First those names would be run through the ICE computer. Later they would show up on the morgue roster.

Dartanian sat at his third floor command post and started pressing buttons that would launch a holocaust in the slaver underground. The war machinery started very subtly when he dispatched two ICE agents to circulate in the bars and spread the word that a reward was being offered for Jerry Cornell's head.

The others were waiting for Dartanian the next morning in Stu's garage in Little India. It was quiet and tense when Dartanian walked in. Stu and Martin had picked up word on the street that Jerry made a move against the other gangs.

They believed him when he said he had nothing to do with it, but like Alex had pointed out the other day, innocence had nothing to do with it. If Jerry's name was circulating on a freelance hit list he was a walking target. Stu and Martin faced the same treatment if they hung with Jerry.

"So now what?" Martin said. "Go to the mats? Hide out or split up? What do you have in mind for us?" He directed the question at Jerry. Jerry looked at Dartanian and the small group understood that leadership of the gang had just changed hands.

Dartanian spoke quietly. "Our best bet is to fight back. But first we've got to get some financing and go on a trip for a few days. Then we come back when the heat dies down and blow the bastards away."

"What if we don't go along?" Martin said.

"If we split now, we're all dead. One by one it'll happen. One day Stu's walking down the street and bam. Maybe you get a slug while you're sleeping, Martin. Maybe this thing dies down and Jerry is in a new line of work when all of a sudden he gets reminded by a bullet in the head."

Martin wasn't too happy with Dartanian's answer, but he read it the same way. He would desert if things got heavy, maybe take up residence in another city. Dartanian knew that Martin was trustworthy as long as it was to his advantage.

"Something else," Dartanian said. "Whoever is doing this might want to move in and take over the territory, or maybe it's just a nice way to rip off some bankrolls, complete with a fall guy. They'll waste Jerry and the rest of us when they're through. That ties up the loose ends and makes everybody think the right guy's got what's coming."

"Are you saying we should find out who's pulling the hits?" Stu asked. "It's impossible, man. It could be anybody."

"They're pretty good, whoever they are," Martin said. "I don't see how we can trace them."

"I guarantee we'll know before too long. You have my word on it."

The men sat around the garage for a while, letting their new situation sink in. Stu heated up some coffee in a rusted silver pot and Martin grabbed a beer from the cooler. Jerry was still pale from yesterday's drunk and took some coffee.

"How are things at your place?" Dartanian said.

"Bad, I think. I've seen some unfamiliar faces around."

"Yeah?" Dartanian said. Two of those unfamiliar faces were ICE agents who loitered around the neighborhood and made sure that Jerry had seen them.

"Somebody's on to you already," Martin said. "Dammit, this is going down too fast."

"Cut out if you want. I think the best thing to do is move Jerry out of his place, and then everybody else move out for a while, until we got our feet on the ground with this gig."

"Why move him out?" Martin said. "He can split now. Leave everything in the dump."

"I got money, I got weapons, and I got a lot of names and numbers back at my place. I need them if we're gonna stay in business."

"You should have gone back and got everything when you saw those guys." Martin was hungry to fix the blame.

"One of those bastards was following me pretty close. I didn't want to hang around."

"Great," Martin said.

"Screw it," Dartanian said. "Let's do it now. We go back there, get Jerry's things, and quit this complaining. We're a team. Let's act like one."

Dartanian glanced at his watch. A few more minutes and it would be time to lead the team into battle.

The black Caddy roared past Great Jones Street and screeched to a stop at the first phone booth on the right. A silver Le Baron stopped behind it. Both cars were loaded with men looking for revenge. The Caddy held six remnants from "Sick Maddy" Glover's crew. The Le Baron carried Clark Bruce and his men, ready for his first test.

Both gangs had been tipped off by phone calls the night before. The voice on the phone promised to lead them to Jerry Cornell.

Though they were expecting a trap, both gangs thought they could crush anything that came after them. They were prepared this time. Besides, the voice sounded legit. The man on the phone said he wanted Jerry Cornell dead and that was a good sign that he might be on the up and up. A lot of people wanted Cornell dead.

Glover's man waited in the booth. He snapped the phone off the hook on the first ring. "You been stringing us along all morning," he said. "Come across, man, or else we're booking out of here."

The voice on the other end laughed, "You're almost in firing range now."

"Give."

"Go down to Houston Street, turn right, and then take your second left," the voice said. "Cornell lives on Thompson Street in the middle of the block. He'll be coming out any second. Don't miss him." Mick Porter hung up the phone and sank into Dartanian's desk chair. His part was done. All he could do now was sit tight and wait for the statistics to come in.

Dartanian had two ICE cars ready to seal off the block the moment the hunting crews turned down Cornell's block. He also had a van painted the same shade of green as Stu's. Once the operation reached the getaway point, an ICE driver would crash the van and abandon it. Not only would it congest traffic, but it would convince the cops that the occupants of the van fled on foot. The ICE agent would be picked up by one of the other ICE cars, and the van with Dartanian would slip away.

Larry LaSalle sat in a parked car a few houses before Cornell's to provide backup assistance if Dartanian got in trouble. It was a typical ICE setup, flexible and thorough, like their leader.

Alex Dartanian sat in the back of the van with his Skorpion M61 clipped and ready. The van was double-parked in front of the brick apartment building where Jerry rented a three roomer. Stu watched the street in front of him and glanced in the sideview mirror every few seconds.

Martin sat in the passenger seat with his elbow out the window, which would serve as a gunrest for his Browning. He tapped the barrel of the Hi-Power on his thigh, nervously keeping a beat to the van radio. It was turned on low, playing a Frank Sinatra song.

The music seemed perfect for the atmosphere. Nothing was going to happen. They were all worried about nothing.

"See anything?" Dartanian said. "Anybody that doesn't belong?"

"Everybody looks like they don't belong to me," Stu said. "What's taking him so long?" Stu was on edge but for him the possibility of trouble was worse than the actuality. Once he wheeled them away, he would be alright, no matter what went down around him.

Dartanian glanced out the tinted half-moon window at the rear of the van. There was nothing in sight, but the time was near so he took out two more clips from the case at his feet.

"Shit!" Stu shouted. "Look at this fucking Caddy!" He saw it in the side mirror. "It's loaded, man. Damn, there's another car with them."

The Caddy slowed down as it approached the van. One man jumped out. The nose of a small pistol was in his hand. He ran towards the steps of the apartment building just as Jerry came out the front door with a loaded backpack swinging in his hand.

"Come on, come on, move your ass," Stu said, looking first at Jerry, then at his mirror. The Caddy hadn't made the van yet but it would any second. The hunters were just looking for Jerry, not a gang.

The man from the Caddy stopped in front of the steps and raised his pistol. Martin blew the back of his head open with a round from the FN Browning.

Stu slammed the van in reverse and angled it onto the curb. It pushed aside the rear of the car parked in front of the building and supplied cover for Jerry. He dived into the side of the van.

The van screeched into the street just as the Caddy roared in behind it. The Le Baron pulled alongside. It's front end rose close to Stu's door. Jerry grabbed an MP40 submachine gun and crouched in the well behind Stu's seat.

Dartanian looked out the rear window and saw the faces of the men in the Caddy. Glover wasn't there. Some other time, Dartanian thought. First the soldiers, then the general.

"Stop the van," Dartanian said.

"What?" Stu said. "They'll get us."

"Slam on the brakes. Now!"

The van jerked to a halt. The nose of the Caddy folded as it hit the bumper. Dartanian pulled the tricked-up lever on the ceiling of the van. Both rear doors shot open instantly and Dartanian popped up like a jack-in-the-box. He knelt on the platform and squeezed the stinger of the Skorpion.

A connect-the-dots line appeared on the windshield as the 7.65mm rounds surprised the life out of Glover's men. Blood splashed onto the windows and the seats. The side door opened and two men tumbled out. Dartanian waved the Skorpion and they hit the cement dead.

He threw another clip into the Skorpion and sprayed the windshield one more time. The windshield dropped in particles and gave Dartanian a clear target. He emptied one last clip inside the car. Death was the only passenger left in the Caddy.

The silver Le Baron had shot past them and now it waited at the side of the road. The driver was uncertain of what to do. They'd come to kill a man, not engage in a battle with a band of fanatics.

Jerry strafed the windows of the Le Baron as the van rocketed past them. The Le Baron crashed into a parked car on the left side of the road. Clark Bruce screamed at the driver to get them away. He was about to do it when a .357 slug changed his mind forever. The driver slumped over the steering wheel.

Clark Bruce looked over to the sidewalk and saw a man with a beard and mustache aiming at him. It was the last thing he saw.

Larry LaSalle walked away.

The throwaway ICE van crashed on cue, a half minute after Stu was gone.

Inside the van, three men were convinced that Dartanian had correctly predicted what would happen to them. They were also convinced that he could lead them out of the bloody mess.

Dartanian looked at the men, flushed with success and adrenalin. He would lead them, alright, one by one until there were none.

—————————— *Ten* ——————————

Hookers at the Regal Motel specialized in ripoffs. The barracks-shaped motel on the outskirts of New York City catered to businessmen who were looking for a good time.

It was a conman's haven. The action was fast, and almost any connection could be made in the motel's dark lounge. The customers, who had been steered to the 'swinging' motel, were made for hustling.

Many a businessman woke in a stupor to find his wallet missing along with the hooker. Some woke with their heads smashed by a bottle, ripped off even before they had a chance to score with the hooker. The cops knew about the sleazy activity, but there were hardly any complaints. The victims didn't want any publicity so they were played for suckers instead of suckees.

Not everybody got burned at the Regal. For some it was home away from home. They belonged there because they were part of the scene. The Regal was a safe place for underworld players. The management was cool to them because they brought in the action and a lot of cash.

Martin was a regular at the Regal. He lived there on and off, depending on his bankroll. It was no problem finding him. ICE agents reported him staying in room 131 of the Regal.

Dartanian sat in a parked car across from 131 for a half hour, waiting for Martin's hooker to leave. It was one o'clock in the morning and the motel was in full swing. He saw expensively dressed hookers take their clients into rooms on either side of 131.

He'd also seen an obvious drug buy when a carload of college boys pulled up in front of one of the lower level rooms. One got out with his hand in his wallet pocket. He disappeared into the room for two minutes and emerged with an ultracool smile on his face. He'd made his buy.

Dartanian couldn't help thinking about the college boy dealing with a real shark someday. Instead of dancing out of a motel room with a few grams of coke, he'd stagger out with a headful of lead.

A 17-year old girl with gleaming platinum hair ran out of one room with just a skirt and an unbuttoned blouse on. She carried high heels and a purse in one hand beating it out of there. A skinny man poked his head out the door and stared after her. "She took my money," he said. Disbelief and regret played on his face and gave way to embarassment. He closed the door and chalked one up to experience.

Light spilled from room 131. The rented lady skipped out of the room. She patted her hair and then adjusted her mouth with a thin gold tube of lipstick.

Ten minutes later the lights went out.

Dartanian glanced up and down the motel walkway and waited for it to clear. Two hours ago he'd read the report on a man named Walkins, who had gotten clobbered when he confronted Martin and Dartanian on the Carol Sutherland grab. Walkins was barely alive. He was confined to a wheelchair and his chances of recovery were slim.

It was time for Martin to go down.

Twenty minutes passed before the Regal quieted down. Dartanian crossed the cracked-tar parking lot to room 131. He stuck a thin steel-tipped pick into the keyhole. The lock was old and cheap. Dartanian applied the right amount of tension on the core lock. It took five seconds to rake it, about the same time for a real key.

The blond man slipped into the room and closed the door behind him. He waited a second for his eyes to adjust and stepped to the center. He heard Martin's deep breathing. He stood over the bed, slid his hand under the pillow for the Browning. It wasn't there. Martin felt secure tonight.

Alex switched on the bedside light.

"What the fuck—" Martin said. His hand shielded his eyes when he sat up in bed. He came out of sleep quickly and threw a punch at Dartanian.

Dartanian batted the fist away.

Martin recognized him then. "Man, you had me scared. For a second I thought my number was up."

"It is."

"What are you talking about, Lex?"

"My name isn't Lex Daniels."

"So?" Martin said. "Who's got a real name these days?"

"My name is Alex Dartanian. Dartanian Security Service. Get the picture?"

Martin glanced around the room furiously as if his eyes could carve another exit besides the one behind Dartanian. He rolled over to the far side of bed. "What is this, a joke? Come on, Lex, what's going on? So you're some kind of private dick." While he talked, he was planning his next move. He looked at the desk by the motel window. The holstered Browning laid next to a broad-based lamp.

"This is about a promise I made this afternoon. I told you that you'd find out who was behind the hits. Now you know."

"I still don't get it," Martin said. He positioned his feet on the floor next to the bed, readying for his dive across the room.

"The cops and the courts can't touch you, Martin. Neither can my security agency. But ICE can. ICE, Martin, listen to it. Inner Court Executions. You've been judged unfit to live, and here's your goddam sentence."

Martin ran across the room. Halfway to his gun, he twisted around and fell to the floor. A three-round burst from the Skorpion put out his lights. The noise from the silenced machinepistol was a bit louder than a cap gun. It was drowned out by a party blasting away from the upstairs level.

Dartanian holstered the Skorpion and stepped out of the motel room. He walked casually to his Audi and drove away from The Regal. The world was a better place without Martin.

One more rung in the ladder had been chopped away. Dartanian felt no guilt. Martin wasn't an innocent. Neither were the other targets in the ICE operation. They had made their choices when they moved into the slavery business and soon they would get their severance pay from ICE.

"They got Martin," Jerry said. He was living out of Stu's garage. It wasn't comfortable but it had enough food and weapons for a while. He drank coffee from a chipped mug on a wooden bench half covered with tools, primer, and a paint gun.

"I know," Dartanian said, sitting across from him. "I saw it in the morning paper." He laughed. "*The Post* called him a talent scout, can you believe it? They theorized he was wasted by an angry starlet who fell for the casting couch routine. He had a phony business card that called him a talent scout."

"How can you laugh?" Jerry said. "They're getting close. Man, we got to move out fast." He drained the mug of black coffee and then fished for a cigarette from a wrinkled pack.

"Relax," Dartanian said. "I got a picture of the girl we're gonna grab." He passed a photograph to Jerry. "Think our man Storm will take her?"

"Oh yes," Jerry said. "She's a looker, man, we'll get a good price from him. But what about a crew? Who can we replace Martin with that we can trust?" He shook his head and puffed hard on the cigarette. He coughed hard. He reminded Dartanian of a speed freak, falling apart nerve by nerve. "We're too weak without a fourth man." Jerry sounded like a kid caught shoplifting, talking to his daddy for a way out. "What are we gonna do?"

"I got a man I worked with in the past. He's solid as they come."

"Yeah. But there's a reward out for our heads. What if he's greedy? Who's got friends at a time like this?"

Dartanian glared at Jerry. "I said he's solid. I worked with him before. You can trust him like you trust me."

"Okay," Jerry said. "That's good enough for me. Let's meet him." Jerry was relieved. Lex knew what to do. He always knew. It was good to have a plan rather than sit around and wait for his execution.

The man Jerry was counting on was engineering that execution from the inside. "Okay," he said. "I have to dig him up. You and Stu meet us in an hour in front of The High Hat. You can check him out then and we'll talk things over."

Jerry nodded.

Stu was silent. He hadn't said a word since Dartanian entered the garage. The hit on Martin surprised him and made him realize how serious things were. Stu poured his nervousness into the van, tuning it and cleaning it with total concentration. After all, the van was the only friend that Stu ever counted on.

An hour later, two men were waiting in front of The High Hat when they spotted the van. It cut through two lanes of traffic and pulled over to the curb.

"This is it," Dartanian said. "Act heavy."

Mick glanced at him. "You putting me on?" Then he walked to the edge of the curb. His huge body was totally relaxed. Acting was something he loved. Mick easily slipped into the persona of a street tough who claimed respect as his birthright. He climbed up into the passenger seat of the van.

Stu gave him the once over. His bald shiny head wasn't covered by the usual cap. The hot afternoon caused the sweat to trickle down his thick neck. He looked like he was on a blind date just getting his first look at the goods.

"S'matter?" Mick said. "You never seen class before?"

Stu nodded. "Yeah, I guess that's it." He didn't perceive any menace from the huge newcomer towards him. He noticed that this guy seemed capable of handling any situation that came up. "Welcome aboard." Mick passed his test with Stu. The new part for the machinery was a perfect fit.

Jerry was glancing up at Mick, studying him like a weapon to judge its caliber.

"What is this? A beauty contest?" Mick said. "Lay off the eyeballing before you lose one of them." Mick had a tendency to overdo his tough guy act, but it was difficult to tell what worked best with these guys. He usually got the best results when he played it dumb but streetwise.

"Sorry," Jerry said. "Just going by the book, man. Got to look you over."

Mick looked at Dartanian who was sitting back against the plushly-lined wall of the van and smiling. "I thought you said this was a sure gig. Do I gotta pass twenty questions with these boys or what?"

Dartanian shook his head. "They like you. I can tell your charm overwhelmed them."

"Exactly," Jerry said.

"Pleasure to be here," Mick said.

Jerry had been worried about bringing someone in so fast, but they needed a fourth man or else any outfit they did business with would be tempted to try a ripoff. Dartanian was calling the shots, and if he said this man was good, that was enough for Jerry. He didn't have time to stop and think about what was happening. He only had time to act and these guys were men of action.

The van cruised leisurely up Park Avenue. The sun baked down on the freshly painted black van. It was a smooth finish, layered and reflective as glass.

"Okay, let's get it straight so we all know what we're in for. Mick, this is Jerry C. He's got about thirty guys looking to slit his throat at the moment and he wants to know if you'll join the party."

"Don't we all," Mick said. "Yeah, I'm in."

"Good," Dartanian said. "And Jerry, Mick gets a full quarter of anything we make. He'll carry out the first grab with me. Later on we can work out different arrangements so you can set up a few chicks of your own to hit. We're gonna do a lot of business. High volume."

Jerry nodded. He liked Lex's attitude. The man went about his business as if there weren't three gangs in the city gunning for him. He kept thinking how any other man might have split a long time ago, and written Jerry off as a corpse. But Lex jumped right in and stood next to him. If the new guy Mick was anything like Lex, nothing could stop them.

They drove around for another half hour and set a time for the grab. Jerry had already told Storm that he had a special delivery coming his way. The Turk was interested and willing to pay a higher price if the goods were high quality, as described.

Jerry's gang was in business again.

Mick and Dartanian got out of the van at midtown.

"How'd I do?" Mick said.

"A little thick," Dartanian said. "Sort of a combination of Wallace Beery and Moose Scholock."

"Yeah," Mick said, "that's what I was trying for."

The two ICE agents went over to the Cage Street headquarters. Dartanian drew up a list of agents for the task force. The move was on. First came Storm, and then Denaud. He was positive that the highest link in the slave chain was Denaud. Jerry felt that way too, but they really couldn't know unless Storm verified their suspicions. Either way, Denaud would get hit. The ICE army was on the move and it wouldn't stop until they found the senator's daughter, no matter how many links that had to break.

The next morning had a "hunt" atmosphere. Four slavers, two bent on destroying this particular slave chain, met at an all-night diner in the Lower Broadway block just above City Hall. It was 4 A.M., still dark, with a summer chill in the air.

After a quiet breakfast they left the diner, eager to hunt while the world slept. Stu drove them to a run-down apartment building up on Third Avenue.

Mick and Dartanian hopped out of the van. It made a quick circuit of the block and then, right on schedule, it stopped in front of the apartment building again. The two men hurried down the steps. They carried a woman in tight black pants and a clinging knit top. She looked like one of the young dancers that flocked to New York, trim, sharp lips and soft face, nice body.

Jerry eased her into the van while Dartanian closed the door behind him. Mick jumped into the front and they were off.

"She's better than her picture," Jerry said. "If we had more time I could get a hell of a price for her."

"We don't have more time," Dartanian said. "We need the bucks now."

"I know, I know," Jerry said. His eye judged the quality of the goods. A wistful look came to his eyes. He stroked her waist and then skipped his fingers over the front of her soft knit top. "Too bad we don't have time to get to know her better."

"That's right," Dartanian said. He settled back for the long ride. By the time they were out of the city it was getting light out.

The woman lying on the platform behind Dartanian was Val Wagner. She was fully conscious to begin with but the best way to keep up the act was to grab some sleep. The throbbing of the van on the Thruway helped ease her into dreams.

She didn't wake up until they left the Thruway at the second Catskill exit. From then on she kept alert. Once they got inside the Turk's compound things were going to happen fast.

Val Wagner had long black hair, a face that was sultry or haughty depending on her mood, and plentiful curves that caused several men to underestimate her ability. That splendid body had been trained to do much more than satisfy a man. Val knew that the best way to a man's heart was a spear hand to the ribcage.

As she lay there quietly, putting up with the occasional hand of Jerry Cornell resting upon her breasts, Val looked like a preferred victim for the slavers. She was 35 but looked 21. She was a beauty, ripe for capture, ready for sale. She was also the only female agent to make it through the ranks of DSS to ICE.

The attractive brunette had assumed many personalities and identities in her work for Dartanian. She was capable of acting as a career woman, a dimwitted actress, or a bored and hungry secretary. She could take dictation, type a hundred words a minute, and blow away a bull's eye with her .38 Smith and Wesson at a hundred feet.

Val was flexible in undercover work. She knew that assumed identities had to go all the way. It wasn't like on television where a the lady cop plays a hooker and never beds anyone. It was a' job. She was a professional. She always got her man no matter how it had to go down.

She had come up through the insurance agencies, learning every phase of the investigations field, and then made the step up to security agencies. Her talents and ambition shot her through until she finally reached the top, DSS, where she found that she wasn't as hot as she thought. Her real training began. She studied under Sin Simara for the deadly arts, and she picked up the ways of a modern security specialist from Dartanian.

Val went on the streets like the other DSS operatives. She worked on the line in every conceivable security situation.

Once they worked with her, the DSS operatives

stopped comparing her to "Charlie's Angels." "Better bring your bikini, Val, there could be trouble ahead."

One day Val worked on a rape decoy trap for a celebrity-studded apartment complex victimized by some "name-hopping" thugs. Three men came at her at one o'clock in the morning with knives. They laughed and didn't think she would shoot.

She showed them, and the world was less a trio of perverts. From that time Val Wagner was no longer considered a "fair" operative, a former brilliant beauty queen from Nebraska. She was a DSS operative. Three firefights later, Val Wagner was taken into the confidence of Dartanian and moved into ICE.

She was born for it, and like the others, would die for it if she had to. ICE agents were committed to waging the war that no one else dared fight.

The van climbed the rear access road that led to Storm's Catskill haven. They stopped at the guardhouse where two of Storm's men snapped out of their mountain-air calm. One guard opened the side door of the van. The other looked in through the passenger side.

The man in the side grinned. "Another piece of candy for Storm's sweet tooth," he said. He stared at the brunette in the back and nodded at Jerry. "Better than the usual tramp you guys bring."

"No," Jerry said. "Just average."

The guard laughed. Each time he saw Jerry make a delivery he loosened up a bit more.

Dartanian looked at him idly, thinking that there wouldn't be a next time for the guards, or for anyone in the compound that sat on top of the peak.

In the woods surrounding the retreat, Sin Simara commanded a small army. There were twelve men with him, the same ones who manned the boats for Jerry's delivery to the Asian connection.

The men were in cammies that blended in with the summer colored forest. They were ready to strike anytime; the schedule called for them to hit when the van went through the guardhouse on the way back.

The van bumped over the next quarter of rock strewn road that prevented a quick entry to the fortress. Storm hadn't counted on a land-based force coming after him. That was unthinkable. A few minutes later the van reached the clearing. There sat finely duplicated chateaus, looking like they had been transplanted from a Renaissance French countryside. They were pleasing to the eye even if they were incongruous with the true nature of the man who built them.

There were no lovelies cavorting around the pool. The most recent batch had just been shipped out. They were on their way up the slave chain.

Dartanian glanced around the compound. There were a half dozen men with arms patrolling the grounds. Some of them were casual, others were on a definite patrol pattern. These were the ones who were visible. The last ICE surveillance of the compound placed the number of men at sixteen.

One of the men flagged down the van as it rolled towards the chateaus. "Right on time," he said to Stu. "Take her in there." He pointed to the square garage attached to the largest building. The large overhead door was sliding open.

Stu drove in. The doors closed behind them, and then Bernard Storm came out to meet them. There was an excited look on his dark complexioned face. "Let me see her," he said, when the side door of the van slid open. He looked inside at the still form of Val Wagner. After studying her, he said, "She is worth the price you quoted."

Jerry got out of the van. Dartanian followed.

A guard pointed a pistol at Dartanian. He stood still, just outside the van. "What is this?" he said.

"Sorry," Storm said. "Security. I can only allow my good friend Jerry to come with me. Word of the troubles in the city has reached me, of course."

"It's okay," Jerry said. "He's the one that saved my ass. We're being set up for a big fall, but Lex is getting us out of it alive. Trust me."

Storm nodded his head.

Dartanian laughed inside. *Trust me.* That was one of the most common sayings among the underworld and the least applicable.

"You can come," he said to Dartanian. "Bring the girl and leave all of your weapons inside."

Dartanian stripped off his holsters and dropped them in the van. He caught Mick Porter's eye and saw that the man riding shotgun had his Ingram M10 resting between the seat and console. He was ready to jump into action. Dartanian shook his head no. He slung Val Wagner over his shoulder. He followed Storm and Jerry, sandwiched between two guards as they moved into the Storm estate.

They moved into a rustic room. It had Storm's fake personality stamped all over it. Plenty of artificial warmth. Rich pine wood sections bordered a fieldstone fireplace, and on the walls were Early American muskets and weapons. It could have been the study of a museum curator, stuffed with expensive memorabilia.

Storm's two guards hung in the background and positioned themselves at opposite ends of the room. Dartanian had a chance to take out the guards if he wanted to. They were dressing, like everything else in the room. It wouldn't take much. There were several articles to use as weapons: fireplace items, pokers, tridents, swords, driftwood encased lamps, and Dartanian's body itself, a deadly arsenal. And there was Val.

It was just a ritual calculation. Dartanian was trained to think in assault terms. There was no need to carry it out, but something for his mind. Dartanian eased Val's body onto one of the bearskin draped couches. Then he and Jerry sat across from the Turk.

"You said you wanted to discuss a matter when we spoke the other day," Storm said.

Jerry mentioned the gangwar in New York, how they were moving against him, how he was framed, and most important, how he wanted to work in another city for a while until things calmed down. It was old news to the Turk. He had more than one man running women to him from the city.

"There's even talk of a reward for me," Jerry said.

"Five thousand," Storm said. "To be precise."

"Right," Jerry said. "So we're splitting north for awhile, and we need work. We're thinking of Montreal, and naturally we hoped you could put in a word with Denaud."

"Denaud?" Storm said. "What makes you think I have anything to do with Denaud?"

Alex marvelled at the man's sheer portrayal of honesty. If ICE hadn't gathered enough material to hang Storm and Denaud, he almost would have believed him. Ever since Jerry first spilled Storm's name, ICE had been working overtime, amassing the crimes of Bernard Storm.

His real name was Bajazet Sorgun and he had credentials with the U.N. as an assistant ambassador at the Turkish embassy and a consultant on international export. He anglicized his name to Bernard Storm for his dealings with Americans who worked in the slavery racket, his only expertise in exporting. Storm moved back and forth from the city to his retreat in the mountains. Corruption was second nature to him. With his immunity, Storm had the entire U.S. as his playground. He was untouchable by laws, but very touchable to the man who sat across from him. Dartanian could reach out and snap his thick neck in one second.

Storm had connections to Denaud and other body brokers, but Denaud was his main customer.

"I've been in the business for years," Jerry said. "I understood that Denaud was the next man in the chain. I could be wrong, but if I'm right, all I'm asking is that you put in a word for us. Maybe he can use us there."

"But why Denaud?" Storm said. "Why Montreal? Not that I can help you, but maybe if you told me a little more . . ."

Jerry shrugged. He looked at Dartanian, then back to the Turk. "Actually, one of the reasons for Montreal is that, uh, I can get a fortune for a girl I sent through the pipeline. A customer got a look at a snapshot I had lying around and flipped. I figure I can trace her and buy her back, sell her to my customer and still make a profit. I also figure Denaud got the chick from you. So that's all there is to it."

"No more lies, Mr. Cornell," Storm said. His cheerful voice faded and gave way to his graveyard manner. The two guards stepped closer and unholstered their automatic pistols.

"What do you mean?" Jerry said.

"The girl you are looking for is Cindy Barrington. You do not want to buy her back. You want to kill her. Don't play games with me."

Jerry dumbly nodded his head.

Storm gave him a brittle smile. "But you come at a good time. I was just about to send a man up there to kill her. At my expense. Now you can assume the burden."

"How'd you find out?"

"After we seasoned her, we sent her out on the circuit. She talked crazy, but they all talk crazy, anything to escape their misfortune, so she was ignored. Shortly after we transferred her to Montreal, word reached me that her rantings were based on fact. Her real name is Cindy Barrington, and she is the daughter of a senator who is most likely burning tracks to us as we sit here. She's legit and your ass is on the line."

The stout Turk glanced over at Val. "Who's she? The president's mistress?" He laughed and Jerry sensed that he was in no danger. Storm had probably heard hundreds of stories from women who all made up reasons about why they should be set free. Cindy was the rare one, a VIP's kid. Another situation couldn't happen in a million years where the chosen girl was hot enough to kill.

"Right," Jerry said. "You've figured it right. We want to go north and hit the chick before it's too late. What the hell, with all of us working on it the chick is sure to get it before Denaud catches on."

"If he does our heads will roll," Storm said. "Starting with you." He looked at Dartanian. "And then you."

"We'll get her," Dartanian said. "You can count on it." *And count on dying today you bastard,* Dartanian thought.

Storm got up. "I'll see what I can do about contacting this Denaud you think I know." He let them sit there while he made a call in the next room. He came back five minutes later. "Denaud is looking for your arrival in his fair city. I told him you were excellent workers with high quality goods."

"Thanks," Jerry said. "I don't know how to repay you for this."

"Oh, a thousand thanks would suffice. Per man, that is."

He took it out of the agreed upon price for Jerry's latest delivery and gave them twelve thousand instead of sixteen. Considering there was a five thousand dollar reward on Jerry's head it wasn't such a bad deal. Storm could have kept the girl, wasted Jerry and the gang, and collected the bonus. There would have been bad blood against him from any of the other slavers that Storm dealt with. Cornell had it coming.

It didn't hurt that Cornell confessed his real reason for going to Montreal to the Turk. Both had the same interest, and if things worked out, their relationship could go on as before.

Eleven

One minute after the van passed through the gates there was a blur in front of the guard's eyes. He fell with a shuriken embedded in his head. The second guard was torn between shock at his partner's spouting blood and fear for himself. He raised his cobalt blue pistol, but didn't get a shot off. A second shuriken whipped through the cool morning air and lodged in his throat. The dull finished metal star acted like a spigot. He tried to remove it but only succeeded in tearing more of his throat. He sank to the dirt in a paling heap.

A swarm of camouflauged men poured through the gates. There were six here, and seven above on the hill. The six men ran full speed through the rocky hillside, noiselessly darting in and out of the trees. A cool breeze kicked at their backs as they headed towards the main camp. Sin Simara had a five-yard lead on the rest of his men, but none were slow. They were conditioned nine days out of ten. They were ICE and nothing could stop them.

Inside the compound, the startled Turk regarded his new companion. She was wide awake and staring at him. This had never happened before. They'd always been drugged long enough for his satisfaction.

"What's the matter?" she said. "Can't handle it when we talk back?"

He stared at her as if she was a ghost. Only a moment ago his hand had patted her breasts. She had jumped away from him as if touched by a snake.

It wasn't fair. This spoiled everything. Storm needed to play with the captives until they awakened from their stupor and slowly realized what was happening. After all, that was the thrill.

Storm was their first stop on a trip into a nether-world of horror. But this one was different. She didn't wake up in the midst of his sexual kink displays. She cheated and woke before he could even start.

He stared at her. He was totally unaccustomed to anyone talking back to him; he had always called the shots.

"I think I know your problem," Val said. "I'm not dead enough for you."

His face reddened. He went through a series of twisted faces, like a man beyond control. "Stop it, stop it, no one talks to me like that!" His massive body thundered across the floor of the cozy little palace.

He was going to teach her a lesson and then take her to the training room. "You aren't going to get out of this alive. The hell with the money. I'll take the loss on you . . ."

Storm had dismissed his armed servants after the van left. He would punish Jerry Cornell for not drugging this one properly. But first he would punish this one himself.

Val laughed at him. He lunged at her, but she stepped away easily. Then he swung at her. Each time she avoided him, and his face became more red. His eyes became more insane, and hatred poured from his deepset eyes. If those monstrous fists touched her, she would be in trouble.

Val was one to the girls who could defend herself. She wasn't drugged and tied, or scared by the greasy sadist.

"If you don't come over here right now, I will not have the kindness to kill you. No, my dear, you will learn that to disobey me is very foolish. I can keep you alive for months . . . and you will wish you were dead."

He waited in the middle of the room. "Come here."

"A pleasure," she said.

Val skipped across the room. Her left foot touched the floor and gave her the momentum for a flying front snap kick. Her right foot wheeled through the air, arcing past Storm's vainly blocking hands, and then her black-toes pump took him under the chin, crunching the trachea.

He fell to his knees and clutched his shattered windpipe. His eyes were the eyes of a man who swallowed a lead pipe.

"I can't breathe," he gasped.

"That's the idea," Val said.

His eyes begged her. The eyes of a killer and sadist who had sent countless numbers of innocent women up the slave chain. He had profited from them and used them in the sickest way possible.

He would have killed her painfully and slowly. She knew that he had meant his threat. Still he hoped his men would come and save him at the last minute.

Storm grabbed for her one more time, hoping to pull

her down to share death waiting for him. She escaped his attempt to grab her throat. Storm rolled over and over on the floor, heading towards a desk in the middle of the room.

Val stepped behind him within striking range. He pulled open a desk drawer and reached inside for a Makarov pistol. His hand touched the butt of the 9 x 18mm defensive weapon a split second before Val's heel jabbed into the back of his hand and shattered his knuckles. Her left foot whipped into his side, burst his left kidney, and followed through with a finishing kick to the back of his neck. Her toes spiked the base of his skull.

Mr. Storm was no more.

The shots that had been going off for the last minute finally registered on Val. She grabbed the Makarov from the top drawer and hurried from Storm's rustic chambers. She walked quietly through the breezeway that connected to the garage and peered inside.

Two of Storm's men stood on either side of the garage door, looking out at the compound through small rectangular windows at eye level. They had AK 47 assault rifles with 30-round clips ready, waiting for the ICE agents to come inside. They hadn't committed to the fight, hoping to surprise the invaders.

Val gripped the Makarov and squeezed off two head shots. As the bodies fell, she fired one more round apiece to make certain they stayed down.

She ran outside and found the ICE team mopping up. Sin Simara and Larry LaSalle swept through the camp, body to body, making sure Storm's men were dead. Red Casey and Tim Reed strafed the compound with their Galil assault rifles.

The fight was over in two minutes. Storm's men were prepared to guard against casual strangers who stumbled unaware into the camp. But they were no match for the elite force of ICE men.

Simara and Val began to search the compound for lists of names, money, and record books that would show Storm's connections. They made one grisly discovery in a hidden room on the lower level of Storm's main chateau. Locked in a dark, stale room was a girl of thirteen. She was wasting away, half crazy from the ordeal she'd been through. Storm had kept her around for his amusement.

The girl panicked when she saw the squad of men in green cammies and the lady in black. Like a bird of prey the young girl fluttered over to the corner of the cell when they entered.

She didn't talk or cry. She just crouched there like a black and blue nightmare.

"That sick bastard," Val said. She reached out her hand to the girl. The girl turned her head away. She stared at Val as if she was expecting something horrible to happen to her. The girl needed help. She needed a hospital. There was a chance she would be able to supply names and faces of those she had encountered at the camp but that wouldn't be for some time.

The ICE team found a safe with $300,000 and a handsomely bound catalog of women, which included hundreds of photographs of women in all conceivable poses, from fully dressed to bound and naked. The catalog was probably used to advertise Storm's collection to potential clients. It stretched back nearly ten years. Val could tell by the varying hair styles.

She looked at the faces that would never smile again. Now they were all over the globe, or maybe in an unmarked grave, disposed of forever. The ICE team collected the weapons lying around and set explosives through the compound.

A short while later, a blast rocked the mountain top. There was a fire on the hill; Bernard Storm and company went up in smoke.

Twelve

Montreal boasted the largest underground city in the world. Miles of shopping malls, movie theaters, restaurants and hotels were connected by the Metro system. It was possible to live year round without seeing the sun. This ultramodern subterranean world stretched from Westmount through Place Bonaventure to Place Ville-Marie.

Another underground flourished in Montreal. It was the type that plagued big cities. While ninety per cent of the natives went about making an honest living, ten per cent went about taking theirs.

No one gang dominated the city. There was too much action for that. Consequently several gangs sliced up the underworld marketplace. Drugs and women were the most profitable and the most fought over. The gangs that ran these rackets were the hardest in the city.

There were also gangs that were so powerful that drugs and women became only part of their business. They had money to branch out into other schemes.

One such gang, perhaps the biggest, was run by Pierre Denaud. The French born vicelord landed on St. Catherine Street in the fifties when it was wide open. At first, he was one more hustler looking for a piece of the action. He ran a few women and sold drugs, but so did many other toughs. There was nothing to make Denaud stand out from the pack until he suddenly became a wealthy man practically overnight. One day he was a small time pimp and pusher, the next day he owned a nightclub in the East End.

Denaud had found the right backer, the right connection. Someone believed in him. It wasn't a belief in his smart business sense, but a belief in his ruthlessness and total dedication to living the good life at the top of the heap, no matter what road led him there.

A man like that was made for grooming. Just as a political candidate is picked at a young age and steered towards the top, Denaud was picked as a vice candidate and put on a rocket to the big time.

Pierre Denaud quickly clawed his way through the cosmopolitan jungle and established his territory. He acquired several nightclubs, more than a hundred women, and he dealt whatever drug was in demand. As the years passed, he no longer had to get his hands dirty and separated himself from daily business. His assistants, Louis Eglise from Marseilles, and Guy Caisse, a French Canadian, took care of the rough stuff. Pierre Denaud was untouchable. Nothing could be traced to him personally.

When a theatrical agency that actually sold women to German and Danish slave rings was busted, rumors that Denaud was involved circulated through Montreal, but Denaud was never connected. It turned out that an acquaintance of Louis Eglise had set up the ring and lured girls from Denaud's nightclubs.

Eglise and Denaud were shocked. No matter how

many times a slave ring was traced to one of Eglise's acquaintances, he was shocked. He didn't know how to pick his friends wisely. And that wasn't punishable by law.

Denaud branched out into areas he had never considered when he started out. It was almost as if he had some omnipotent advisor guiding his career and investments. He gained control of a armament company and began exporting state of the art weapons to new corporations springing up all over the world. The strange part was that the corporations usually went out of business right after they received a large shipment of weapons, but that didn't slow his business down. New corporations sprang up as fast as the others died.

By 1980, Pierre Denaud was no longer sure of his holdings. Companies were bought in his name, but he never saw any income and he didn't know what they manufactured except that it had to do with electronics. It was out of his hands, controlled by his backer. Denaud didn't mind, however. He signed his name to the legal papers and washed his hands of it. All he cared about was the money that came from his real businesses, women and drugs.

Occasionally Denaud would ship some women out without getting any payment, following the backer's instruction. The women were sent to places like Afghanistan and the Balkan countries. Eglise said the women were for Soviet troops, since the locals couldn't be trusted. Bordello broads, he called them. Denaud didn't bother to speculate. Whatever the backer wanted, he got, no questions asked.

Denaud began contributing large amounts to Communist fund-raising groups in France in the seventies that mirrored the actions of the corporations. They usually sank without a trace after the donations came.

The backer was bigger than Denaud could imagine. Whenever a representative of the backer visited Denaud, he got first-class treatment and a blank check.

Denaud didn't mind. He went about his business. They had put him on top and he owed them any favors they requested. He went about his business. He was a king in the court of crime, and life was good. As long as he stayed in the good graces of his backer, he had nothing to fear.

Alex Dartanian glanced through the Interpol file on Pierre Denaud in his suite at the Ritz-Carlton. The hotel was elegant and old worldly. The rooms were large and spacious, a welcome change from the cramped van and the plane.

He and Mick had flown into Mirabel International two hours earlier. Stu and Jerry had driven the van up the Northway and were probably at the Canadian border at this very moment. Three ICE vehicles were behind them. ICE was moving north and soon they would all gather in Montreal. Dartanian had attached himself to a DEA operation working on a drug ring from Toronto to Montreal to New York City. It was for cover purposes only, in case the Canadian authorities tumbled onto Dartanian's men. Alex had the DEA cruiser and V-plane speedboat coming down the St. Lawrence River. Both were stocked with weapons and ICE agents. Tim Reed was in charge of the river operation.

Jerry and Stu complained about leaving their weapons behind when the gang split north of Albany, but Dartanian didn't want any trouble at the border. He promised Jerry that his Montreal connections would have weapons waiting for them. He didn't tell him that very shortly those weapons would be used on him.

While he waited for the troops to arrive, Dartanian

reviewed the information on Denaud. Aside from Interpol files, the DEA had plenty, as did the Bureau of Alcohol, Tobacco, and Firearms and the Customs Service. The agencies had been attracted by Denaud's drug and arms deals that spanned the globe. While those agencies went about gathering the information, Alex Dartanian went about acting upon it. The ICE computer had assimilated the information on Denaud into one dossier, but Dartanian liked to consult the original sources when he had time.

From all of the files, it appeared that Denaud worked with several groups that bought his merchandise and services, but his largest and oldest customer was an outfit known as BLOC. It was a consolidation of several corporations and agencies with strange histories. Sudden liquidations of a company's assets and a high rate of suicides in the executive ranks seemed a constant for BLOC. The conglomerate had gone public under the name BLOC in the past year. There was nothing unusual in the actions of the mother corporation, and there were several respected international businessmen on the governing board. By nature conglomerates were volatile entities.

It was the subsidiaries of BLOC that engaged in suspicious activity. Swindlers and disreputable politicians, many formerly holding office in the U.S. served on the subsidiaries. More than thirty subsidiaries dealt with Denaud at one time or another, long before they were gathered under the BLOC umbrella.

Corporations and corruption were old news to Dartanian. It was no surprise that Denaud did business with some shadier branches of the conglomerate.

The first two days of the Montreal phase were spent getting oriented to the city. ICE agents roamed in and out of the melting pot neighborhoods and paid particular attention to Denaud's townhouse in Old Montreal. They visited his nightclubs and counted the men he had available. Several of the agents made trips into the countryside northeast of Montreal where Denaud lived the life of a country squire.

Everywhere Denaud went he was followed by an ICE agent, from his club to his celebrity friends scattered throughout the city. Pierre Denaud was a socialite and half the fun of being a king was being seen and admired.

Larry LaSalle became a regular in Les Dames where the Barrington girl had been spotted. He landed the assignment because he looked like the type to hang around in a strip joint with his beard, mustache, and lowlife eyes. Years of working undercover had trained him for the position.

It was tempting to move against Denaud as soon as Cindy was located. It would have been simple to grab her and run, like ninety-nine percent of the security outfits would, but Dartanian had more than one client. Beside Cindy, there were other women enslaved by Denaud, who would feel the heat when Denaud responded to the grab. He didn't want to spook him before it was time.

When Dartanian moved, Denaud was going down all the way, from the top of his organization to the bottom. There wasn't going to be anything left that could start the chain again. Cindy would keep for a little while longer.

If ICE didn't wipe him out, the slaughter would go on and on and a thousand more Cindys would suffer while lizards like Denaud fed on their blood and tears. Dartanian had to make an example of Denaud and show that the feared slaver wasn't invincible. The assault would come soon, but not until he had all of his troops in place.

Dartanian kept Jerry and Stu in the dark, convincing them he was working on getting their weapons and a fix on the Barrington girl. He had them stay in the French core of the city at the Nelson Hotel where the young tended to gather. Most habitues of the area were card-carrying members of the artistic life, hustlers, and the two New Yorkers blended in well.

Dartanian kept his contact with Jerry to a minimum, using the excuse that he had fled Montreal with gunsights looking for him and had to keep a low profile.

"Contact Denaud when we're ready to move in," Dartanian had told him. "When we have the guns and the muscle, then we hit the chick, if she's still around. Who knows? If things work out alright, we might be able to do some business for him. Relax, enjoy the vacation while you can."

Jerry went along with the plan even though he wanted the problem solved immediately. So far, everything that Lex did worked out. Why should this time be any different?

Master Wu's dojo was fair sized. The polished wooden floor was half the length of a basketball court. Three sides had windows reaching from waist high to the ceiling, looking down on St. Catherine Street. There was an old desk and a changing room in the corner. The desk was piled high with Chinese newspapers.

Master Wu walked up and down a double line of students practicing forms. Occasionally he struck one to test balance. A muscular teenager grinned as Master Wu approached. He had the body of a wrestler and eyes that said nothing could budge him. He was new to the class.

Master Wu tapped him with a back fist that moved no more than six inches. The wrestler staggered several paces back and then landed on his butt. There was a fist-shaped red mark on his chest.

The advertisements in the Montreal papers listed the classes as kung fu, but only because that was the most familiar term to the Western mind. In reality Master Wu taught a martial art based on kung fu moves, but primarily based on punching techniques. It was called Righteous Harmony Fists and first attracted attention in 1900 when the practitioners led the Boxer Rebellion. The Chinese Boxers were of a mystical and fanatic bent with a secret society heritage, and the masters were rumored to perform miracles.

Master Wu had never reached the stage where he could perform miracles, but he was something of a rogue. For one thing, he smoked tobacco. He also drank a bit after his workouts, and he liked to have a good time.

It was three o'clock in the afternoon and Master Wu was demonstrating the use of a short sword to his students, when he saw a Japanese face pass by the open door to his dojo. One blink and he was gone. Master Wu cut short the demonstration and went out to the hallway. It was empty. Across from him was the open door of an office furniture supplier and further down the hall a textbook company. There was no sign of the Japanese man.

Master Wu, known as K'ang Chun in his Taiwan intelligence days, was curious. Was it the same Japanese face that hired him to do contract work for the CIA in Thailand? Was it the same man who launched attacks on the opium dealers in Viet Nam who supplied the American troops with cheap drugs?

Master Wu handed his class over to an assistant, lit a cigarette, and dressed in his street clothes. He walked to Chinatown and soon turned onto Lagauchetiere West. A slender man stood in the pagoda-shaped phone booth outside the restaurant on the corner.

Master Wu smiled and climbed the double flight of stairs to the main dining room. A minute later, sitting in a curved red-cushioned booth with a Gauloise in his hand and a half-finished drink, the white-haired man saw the Japanese man approach.

"Master Wu."

"Master Simara."

The white-haired teacher motioned for Simara to sit across from him. Sin Simara smiled at the man, casually puffing at his cigarette. "Those things will kill you," he said.

"Perhaps. Or perhaps an old friend will toss me into some intrigue from the past and—" The old master slit his throat with his index finger and laughed.

Simara had last seen Master Wu years ago when mainland China waged a covert war against Taiwanese agents abroad. Wu was number one on the hit list. Though he had separated from Taiwan intelligence, Master Wu was still a potent ally. His past included a stint as a double agent in the Social Affairs Department, China's highest intelligence agency. He had been a guerrilla leader against the opium carriers from China to Nam, and he had worked against the SAD in their African subversion campaigns.

Master Wu carried too much information about the Red Chinese for their security purposes. Three Chicom agents, posing as reporters for the New China News Agency had been dispatched to Montreal to hit Master Wu. Simara had been there with him in his apartment, waiting to waste the Chicoms when China suddenly called off the operation. Detente had struck again and they called off their covert war. The publicity would make them look bad.

Master Wu lit another Gauloise. "What dragons are you slaying this time?" he said.

"It is a matter of honor," Simara said. "I could use some honorable men to assist me in an operation. It wouldn't hurt if they could kick a little ass in the bargain."

"I would like to help. But I am retired for good this time. I have a young wife, students, and enough vices to keep me happy."

"Your students . . ." Simara said.

"No. They are clerks, accountants, and college kids. Some would perform admirably. Others would faint in a real fight, nothing but shadow warriors. None are what you seek."

Simara nodded. "I need men capable of creating a diversion and staying put if things get rough."

Master Wu gave him the name of a group in Chinatown that still hadn't found their niche. There was hardly any territory left when they arrived and their turf was a sidestreet lined with old gray deserted buildings and a makeshift clubhouse.

"I don't know if they'll work for you," Master Wu said. "Their leader has a habit of making poor choices. But if they do work for you, they can be counted on. They are hungry and they could use the bread."

"Shall I mention your name?" Simara said.

Master Wu thought for a moment. He looked as though he'd fallen asleep or into the nirvana that Boxers always bragged about. Finally he looked at Simara with a glint in his eye. "Yes, mention my name. It will do you some good."

A few hours after Simara left Master Wu, he walked Montreal after dark. The city had changed subtlely. The tourists sought good times, but were more cau-

tious. The summer sky was meaner and there were
dark shadows caused by the jigsaw architecture.

Sin Simara was avoided by the few street people
who checked him out to see if he was worth hassling.
Once they saw his eyes, they looked the other way.
Simara's customary black clothes were ideal for night-
wear and work. He was ready for action, and that
readiness walked ten steps in front of him.

He walked down the long east-west strip, dotted
with Chinese restaurants and specialty stores that
were closed for the night. Simara explored Clark Street
and then went up and down the old side streets
crammed with apartment buildings that were a mix of
gothic architecture and Chinese pagoda flourishes.
There were several martial arts supply stores and
studios and a few authentic Chinese markets.

Then there was Ward Street, home of the Tai Boys,
a gang led by Kim Huk. Simara turned around the
corner and headed down the block. A Chinese youth
scrambled from a weathered stoop and confronted
him.

"You are lost," he said.

Simara laughed and walked on. The young man
tried to stop him, but somehow the Japanese man
passed. Simara was on the Tai Boys' turf and he
realized that they had to be hungry and desperate. It
was nothing but abandoned commercial buildings and
shantytown apartment houses.

As he walked down the street, other Tai Boys came
out in twos and threes from the alleys and stoops of
Ward Street. Something was happening in their neighborhood, and they were all alert. A stranger. A Japanese stranger had crossed into their territory. Two of
the Tai Boys plunked directly in front of him. "What do
you want?" one said.

"I am looking for Kim Huk," Simara said. He brushed

through the center of the two men, who had both assumed defensive positions that nothing should have been able to penetrate.

Another man might have been scared at the sight. The Tai Boys had gathered *en masse,* hurrying down the street in their bright, blue-sleeved baseball jackets to the center of their street. They stood in front of a freshly painted two-story apartment house that seemed out of place from the rest of the street.

Standing on the porch was a man with a scarred, busted face that had seen a lot of fighting, although he was only twenty or so. This had to be Kim Huk. Master Wu's description emphasized the face and the unusually tall frame of the gang leader.

"You have got yourself lost," Kim Huk said. "But you didn't listen to my man's direction's. That's not very smart. This is our block."

There was an etiquette among gangs the world over. The right name, the right password could guarantee safe passage through a gang's turf. Simara used the password. "Master Wu sent me."

It happened fast. The Tai Boys on the sidewalk formed a semi-circle behind Simara. Kim Huk skipped down the steps and landed firmly on the cement in front of the Japanese intruder. He planted his left foot in front of him and then whirled around with a spinning back kick. Kim Huk's right foot was an inch from Simara's face when his hands shot out in a praying mantis motion that pushed the foot over his head. Kim Huk screamed from the stretching pain in his crotch. Simara's hands imprisoned the foot another second to let Kim Huk see how vulnerable he was.

Simara snapkicked at the man's crotch, but diverted the kick at the last instant and struck his thigh. He pushed higher on the trapped foot at the same time and sent Kim Huk tumbling onto his back.

The Tai Boys were stunned by Kim Huk's failure. The stranger so effortlessly blunted the attack that Kim Huk's ego and reputation were on the line. This street was his and he couldn't abide being handled so easily.

Kim Huk stood and faced him. He raised his left foot so that his toes barely touched the sidewalk like a horse pawing the ground. His back leg bent at the knee. It was simultaneous offense and defense at the same time. With his left hand and left foot forward and his right cocked at his side, nothing could get through it except power. Kim Huk charged and found out what the word power meant.

Simara's sidekick pushed through the snapkick that came at him, through the blocking left hand, and through the layers of muscle of Kim Huk's stomach. The tall man doubled over and flew backwards several feet. When he landed this time, he couldn't get up right away.

The Tai Boys behind Simara attacked. He spun around with a reverse crescent kick that took one man out and jammed him into a second attacker. The instant his right foot touched ground, Simara's left foot pinwheeled out in a regular crescent kick that swept his third attacker's face around in a half circle.

Simara danced and moved between the other Tai Boys who came at him. All were experienced in the arts but none landed a telling blow on the Japanese man. The dance led to the corner. By that time, the Tai Boys realized that Simara was sparing them. He hadn't struck a crippling blow to any man, though they had pulled nothing in their attacks.

Simara stood on the street corner across from the empty park and monument. In the distance, trees covered the mountain that gave Montreal its name. It was not a pleasant place to confront a Chinese street gang, so still, dark, and dangerous.

"The next man dies," Simara said. "No more games."

The Tai Boys stopped. Kim Huk pushed through their ranks, amazed that Simara was in one piece. "You gave no choice," he said to Simara. "I wouldn't have attacked you but you insulted me on my own territory."

"How so?" Simara said.

"You said Master Wu sent you. Master Wu is no friend of mine."

Simara smiled. "He told me his name would guarantee safe passage and introduction to you."

The air had changed. There was no longer the mood of combat. There was curiosity about the newcomer and his reason for coming.

They talked and moved to the center of the street where Kim Huk lived. On the porch, Kim Huk told him about his relationship with Master Wu, how he trained under the old man, challenged him in class one day, tiring of his slow, repetitive teaching. The challenge became real, and the hotheaded Kim Huk ended up in the hospital.

He spread word through the rest of the Tai Boys that he would seek vengeance on Master Wu. The day he got out of the hospital, Master Wu waited for him. He asked if Kim Huk still wanted revenge. Kim Huk swore and attacked. Master Wu put him back in the hospital.

Ever since then there had been enmity between them.

"You are the only one who carries on the war," Simara said. "He was teaching you a lesson."

"He tried to kill me."

"If he tried to kill you, you would be dead." Simara laughed. "Tell me, what have you done since?"

"I have practiced and practiced so I can win the next time."

"He made you a warrior, Kim Huk, forced you to work on your own. In time your hate will turn to power and your vengeance will harden into wisdom ... That, or Master Wu will break your face again."

Kim Huk brushed his long hair back from his face. "But why did he send you here? I thought it was a challenge again. That's why I attacked you."

"No damage done," Simara said. "At least on me." He looked around at the Tai Boys and saw a blackened eye here and there. Simara thought about the way Master Wu operated. The man knew that the Tai Boys would not follow a stranger, especially not a Japanese, if he just came out of the blue. But if he demonstrated his ability and earned their respect, perhaps they would follow. He explained Master Wu as best he could to Kim Huk.

"Why do you think we can be hired?" Kim Huk said. "We are not gangsters. We are a family and we do what is good for the family."

Simara nodded. "It is an honorable matter," he said. "And it is profitable. It will help your family." He envisioned them becoming a force akin to the Guardian Angels that picked up the gauntlet in New York City subways and protected the public.

"We will decide if it is honorable," Kim Huk said.

Simara gave him the name of the target and recited the man's crimes. Kim Huk was familiar with Denaud's operation. "That is suicide," he said. "What happens when you are gone and Denaud strikes back?"

"When I leave there will be no more Denaud."

Kim Huk sensed something deeper about the Japanese man, something that was part of a noble plan, more grand than anything he could imagine. Here was his chance to be a part of it.

"The Tai Boys will help you, I am sure. We will talk it over and give you our answer." They went into the freshly painted house, the club headquarters. Simara saw that it was a family. There were women present, but they weren't promiscuous and wild like their counterparts in New York gangs. They were traditional and stayed in the background while Kim Huk and his men discussed the proposition with Simara.

"But why us?" one of Kim Huk's men said.

"Because I need scary guys," Simara answered. "But I didn't want monsters."

Simara was invited to spend the night in the Tai Boys' headquarters. He slept on the second floor where several cots were prepared. From one of the small bedrooms down the hall ancient Chinese classical music played on a tape player. Lute music filled the house. Simara had become a member of the family. Now he had to look after them.

As he allowed himself to drift to sleep he thought of Master Wu's craftiness. It was like seeing a mirror image thirty years in the future.

Thirteen

She couldn't live without pills. The bright ones gave her energy and the dark ones brought her down. They helped Cindy Barrington live through hell. She couldn't imagine getting along without them.

It was better to stumble through the days with little consciousness. Darvons, Nembutals, and other illegal drugs were hers for the asking. Nothing was too good for Denaud's girls.

Cindy Barrington laid down on her velvet bedspread in the middle of the afternoon. She didn't know what she was on today, except that the pills took the edge off. They were shiny brown capsules without a name imprinted on them, skimmed from a midnight batch at a pharmaceutical company. Mixed with a tall glass of hard liquor the pills put her in never-never-land. No pain, thoughts, or complaints.

She looked around her room. It was soft blue and everything seemed to have a lustrous finish to it. There was a wooden dresser filled with finery the clients liked to see her wear. There was a vanity with a heart-shaped mirror in the room's center. The left-hand top drawer held her cosmetics; The right hand top drawer held her pills. They made her the perfect date for a night on the town.

Cindy laughed on the bed, head sunken into the pillow, eyes staring at the cracked ceiling. Pillhead, she thought. Pillowhead. Pillhead. She toyed with the words repeatedly, laughing dully each time. She didn't have to think about the woman she used to be or the one she had become. The pills didn't allow her to think.

She rolled over and reached down the side of the bed for her cigarettes on the floor. She lit a cigarette and tossed the smoldering match on the rug. What did it matter?

Smoke rings puffed from her mouth and cracked halfway up to the ceiling. Cindy tried to make one reach the ceiling, but she never could. She was getting better though. Soon she would do it; wouldn't that be great.

The room's air was stale. Cindy kept the dark curtains closed over her barred window. She didn't like to be reminded that there was an outside world. She wasn't part of it. With the curtains closed, the pills working, and whiskey, Cindy sank into a pleasant numbness.

Sometimes when the whiskey and the pills hit, she dreamed she was in suspended animation, that she was travelling through time and space on a giant mothership. Everything else was a dream. The faces were not real. Those laughing faces belonged to hard bodies that smashed her around. Sometimes there was more than one man at a time. That was when she was thankful for the pills.

When she first got dragged into Denaud's operation, she heard talk of "battery girls". They were so charged on liquor and addictive drugs that their flesh and minds were totally pliable. The "battery girls" were used for parties where groups of men had the girls at the same time.

Cindy was becoming a "battery girl". She couldn't stop at this stage. She needed drugs and fog. She was evolving into the slaver's idea of a perfect woman.

On the outside, she was young and attractive. The body that lured the men and brought in high bids was in perfect shape, full, soft, and yielding. Inside she was dark and vacant.

There were periodic shocks, moments of awareness when she caught a glimpse of the woman that used to live in this body. A senator's daughter. A senator who was no longer part of her world. She thought of calling him, but every time she wanted to she got a pain in her head. It was the conditioning. The promise of death had been kept often enough so Cindy was no longer capable of trying to escape. She would not use the phone and on the street she would not go to a policeman. Nothing could stop Denaud from reaching out and punishing her once and for all.

The will to survive kept her going. On some level that was submerged in her consciousness, her instinct for self preservation was operating. She did what she had to do to go on living.

She brushed her red hair endlessly. She applied her makeup and glistening body oils that glowed under the stage lights.

Once she had been taken out to Denaud's estate in the countryside. She and another girl supplied the entertainment for Denaud's celebrity friends. Some were actors and some were singers. All were pain, in the ass.

Cindy and the other girl, a cute Oriental with waist length raven hair, had been passed around like meat on a platter to men *and* women. Cindy passed out by the swimming pool. She woke to a scream that echoed inside her head for hours; it was chilling.

In the morning there was no sign of the Oriental girl, and Cindy was delivered back to her third floor cell above the strip joint. She never mentioned it to anyone, but she remembered how the celebrities had gathered in the middle of the night, their worried voices carried to the pool. Cindy pretended to be completely out of it, although the memory came to her in her nightmares.

Cindy lit another cigarette, took another drink, and tried not to think about tonight's performance. She was becoming that mindless creature named Lana that appeared on the posters outside Les Dames. With the costume, make-up, and unworldly painted face on the poster, there was little connection to the beaten creature who sat in her room drugged to oblivion. She was becoming Lana, the person her trainers molded from the raw material of beauty. Their sculpting tools were fear and punishment. The stripper was their creation.

Two floors below, Jerry Cornell sat in the private office of Pierre Denaud. He had seen the poster of the redhead on his way in and had established that she was still here. She had not spoken of her real identity to Denaud. He would run circles around the Canucks. The stripper was going to be wasted before a slip of the tongue wasted him.

All Jerry had to do was work his way into Denaud's crowd, and then hit the chick. It was a shame. She was beautiful. Even though he had slept with her several times in the past, and even though she was a danger to him, Jerry desired her. *Stop thinking with your dick*, he scolded himself. He had to be clear and sharp to get around Denaud. He was a real heavy-weight, and he wasn't in the best of moods.

· Pierre Denaud looked across his long wooden desk at the brash man who'd telephoned him a short while ago. The man was in a rush. He had to see him. Well, now he would pay for his insolence. Denaud smiled. He was amused at Jerry's discomfort. Denaud was gray on both sides. Silvery streaks ran through his hair from front to back, like carefully dyed stripes. He took pains to appear dapper and distinguished. He was a self-made man and he wanted the world to know. Even strangers.

"I don't see what you can do for me," Denaud said. "I have my own carefully selected men. And you come with good reference; I have no need for you."

Jerry nodded. "I hate to waste your time," he said. "I think it would be profitable to you in the long run." He spoke as if Denaud was an upperclass gentleman instead of an expensively-dressed hood.

It was a cat and mouse game. Denaud obviously had something on his mind and when he spoke, it was like he was doing Jerry a favor, talking down to his level. He avoided making any commitments about Jerry's offer to work for him, no matter how many times Jerry asked him.

Jerry realized that Denaud was killing time. He tolerated Jerry's presence for some ulterior motive and didn't try to hide his boredom. Why keep him here? Jerry thought. For a moment he thought of Stu and felt uneasy. He and Stu arrived together after Denaud agreed to see him. The minute they arrived Denaud said, "You and I will talk." A broad shouldered man ushered Stu away. "Louis will entertain your friend while we discuss business."

The man called Louis was probably questioning Stu right now, Jerry thought. That was no problem. Jerry had rehearsed Stu well, and as Stu understood it, the real purpose in coming to Montreal *was* to find work until things cooled off back home.

If he were being questioned while Denaud casually probed Jerry for information, it meant that Storm's word wasn't worth the money Jerry had paid. The introduction was a bust. Denaud didn't trust Storm and denied knowing him. They were the same, Jerry thought, when they said black they meant white.

"This Storm fellow you keep mentioning," Denaud said. "I must tell you I don't know him. I've heard the name, but I have no connection to him. Since you have travelled so far however, I am willing to listen."

Jerry shrugged and sipped the sherry that Denaud had politely offered him. He hated the sweet-tasting liquid, but when among gentlemen, even fake gentleman, it was best to play by their rules.

He looked around the office. It was businesslike. The long desk had three phones and to the left, below a painting of the Montreal World's Fair, was a bank of filing cabinets. It was crisp and air conditioned in the office, a welcome change from the mid-June heat outside.

"Mr. Storm and I had an arrangement," Jerry said. "For several years I supplied certain commodities, which were then sold around the world at high prices because of their tremendous quality. I was the best in New York City."

"How nice for you," Denaud said.

"Mr. Denaud, I would like to talk straight if I may. We both know what I'm talking about. I supplied women. Storm supplied them to the next level, which benefits a good deal from them. I think I have noticed one of my recent women here, headlining at this very club."

"All strippers look alike," Denaud said. "Perhaps

you're mistaken." He affected a look meant to chill the talker and make him change the subject.

Jerry sighed. He had gone through the motions. Cindy was here. They couldn't work from the inside, so it would have to go down the hard way. Lex's alternate plan called for a hit on Denaud's entire operation. He noticed Denaud studying him and gave it one more try because it was expected.

"I can offer my services to you, Mr. Denaud. I can bring you the best women no matter where I work. Here, New York, abroad. Whatever you say."

"Is that why you came here?" he said. He tapped his fingers on the desk. Bored. His eyes said that he was interested in Jerry's response. Denaud obviously knew something, but how much? Jerry wondered if Storm had told him about the wars in New York. Perhaps Denaud had heard it from other sources.

"Things are a little hot for me in New York," Jerry said.

"I see. You are hot, so automatically that should make me want to hire you."

"It's a frame," Jerry said. "Some rival gang was making a big move and hit some other teams working the chick farming business. They all think I called the shots."

"Aha," Denaud said. "So I should be happy to hire a group that turns tail and runs at the first sign of trouble?"

Jerry shook his head. He couldn't win. "I can give you what you want," he said. "We can work direct."

"In other words . . ." Denaud said. "You have eliminated the middleman, eh?" He stared at Jerry strangely, looking for a certain type of reaction.

"Hey, I'm not trying to cut anyone out."

Denaud waved his words away with an impatient hand. "For the sake of argument, suppose I am in the business you mentioned. Suppose I knew this Storm and suppose you had dealings with him."

Jerry nodded.

"Good. Now I shall spell things out for you, eh. Consider me as the Duke, and Storm is one of my lords. What does that make you? An underling, a serf, a peasant. The reason for having a middleman is to save me time wasted on fruitless dealings with small timers like you."

Jerry stood and leaned over the desk. Denaud was certain that he was cowering since he sat so long. There was no need to hide his feelings now. No deal was coming.

"Small time, your ass," he said. "Dukes and lords, is it? Face it, we're all the same. You've had more time at it, but you sure as hell travelled the same road as me. Your fucking highness!" Jerry headed to the door. "You want some real workers, come and find me. And don't bother with the fairy tales."

He twisted the doorknob.

It wouldn't open.

Denaud smiled. He pressed a buzzer under the desk. There was something weird behind the smile. Jerry had told him off, and he got nothing but a smile. "Enjoy your stay in Montreal," Denaud said. The door opened.

Jerry stood in the hall. He walked to the bar, expecting to see Stu sitting with a beer in hand. He would probably have a half-bored, half-angry look on his face from sitting about wasting time when he could be tuning up the van or polishing the new black finish.

The bar was empty. Jerry was about to go back into Denaud's office when he saw Louis. "Where's Stu?" he said.

Louis shrugged. "Out in the van. He didn't like my

company, I guess." Louis walked past him and knocked on Denaud's door.

Jerry went out the front entrance to look for the van. He saw the high gloss shining at the end of a narrow alley. It wasn't wide enough to fit a car into. It was a slice of air space between the stripclub and the limestone building that housed an X-rated filmhouse next door.

Jerry smiled. Chances were that he'd find Cindy on the screen. Denaud's place was the first stopoff on the marketing machine. Brought to the city, trained, filmed for a few of the hardcore epics, and put to work stripping before she was sold to another body broker . . . poor Cindy.

He felt ashamed at the failure of the mission. If Lex had come with them, he would have talked Denaud out of his top hat and would have been part of the inner circle. Lex knew how to do things. He was a first-class persuader. Screw it, Jerry thought. It didn't work out the way he wanted. So what? He just had to play the cards fate dealt him.

There were four cars in the back parking lot of Le Dames. The van was parked in the middle. Jerry slammed the back of the van as he passed, a signal they could get on the road.

Stu was sleeping with his cap over his eyes and nodding forward. He reached over and shook him. "Hey, some backup you are. What if I had trouble in there?"

Stu's head turned towards him. His neck was cut in two. Blood had run down the front of his black work shirt and seeped down his beer gut, where it pooled above his belt.

There were other marks on his face. Stu's cheeks were beat black. There was no time to grieve. Jerry opened the passenger door. Someone kicked it closed.

He saw one of the men who'd been hanging around the bar holding an automatic pistol against the window. Another man stood behind him.

Louis appeared on the driver's side. Behind him was Pierre Denaud.

"Don't say a word," Denaud said. "Storm is dead. Wiped out. I don't know if you did it or not. I don't know if you started that mess in New York. I don't know how many guys you got with you. But I know this. You and every man with you is going to end up like your pal, eh? . . . *If you're behind this.* If not, no hard feelings." He turned and walked away.

Louis Eglise nodded at Jerry. "He was a tough bird. Too bad he had to get it. Now get your ass out of here before you join him. Take him with you."

Jerry reached under the passenger seat. His pistol was gone. The man at his window opened his jacket so Jerry could see it sticking out his inside pocket. Lex had given it to him in case of trouble, and he didn't have a chance to use it.

He pulled Stu into the back of the van and wrapped a blanket around him. Then he numbly started the van and drove off. He was in a daze. He was in Montreal in an area he didn't know well, and he had a dead body in the car. The van was a hearse. Jerry drove around until he found a parking garage. It wasn't the best thing to do, but he would be fried if he got stopped. Jerry was on automatic pilot, his plan being to save his ass one minute at a time. He had to dispose of the van. He smiled at the ticket man and drove to the fourth tier of the garage. He parked in a slot at the back behind a series of circular pillars. He locked the doors and hurried out.

Back in the sunlight, Jerry tried to blend in with the street crowds. It didn't work. He wasn't natural. The last of his original gang was gone. It was up to him,

Lex, and Mick. They would have to make Denaud's fear come true and move against him.

Jerry got lost in Montreal. After walking around the Main for a half hour, feeling naked, vulnerable, and alone, Jerry took a taxi to the hotel where Lex was staying. He called—Lex always demanded an advance call because he was security conscious—and told him he was in the lobby.

"What is it?" Lex said.

"Stu," Jerry said. "For no reason at all."

"What about Stu?"

"They cut him to pieces."

Louis Eglise left his mistress in a bad temper. He paused in the hallway outside her flat. It was a trendy and expensive love nest on St. Denis. The artists had been living in this section for years and it was chic. Chic meant big bucks, and to Louis Eglise, it had been worth it . . . in the beginning.

Marie Levy, the witty cinema star and sometimes a supreme pain in the ass, no longer cared for him properly, especially after a day like today when he had to take care of that guy in the van. It was nice having the face and the body of the screen star in bed with him, but he no longer had her mind. She was becoming independent. Marie had forgotten who built the rungs on the ladder to success that she climbed so rapidly. For a moment, Louis thought of going back inside and really letting her have it, but then he shrugged. He would take care of her in public at some fancy restaurant and show her how much he was in charge.

The princess said he was too old tonight. She wanted someone she could relate too. She wanted to spend time with her peers. "You mean you wanna go work in a whorehouse?" Louis said, and that started the fight.

She turned up the radio. CHOM—the rock station for hip folks. She knew it drove him crazy. It made Louis get up and leave. His hand was on the doorknob. Maybe he would go inside and take her into the bedroom with all the fancy tapestries and candelabras and . . . No, he thought. He wouldn't go back tonight. She would think he needed her.

Louis walked down the carpet and opened the main door that led to St. Denis. At that moment, he saw a striking-looking man walking up the steps in a hurry. Was this one of her peers or lovers? He had the eyes and the face of a model, the build of an athlete, all packed into a nicely tailored blue pinstripe suit. Yeah, this was Marie's type, he thought, someone she *related* to.

That's her game he thought. She gives him a toss for the money he shells out on her pad and her real lover shows up, some pretty boy from central casting. Maybe he'd show pretty boy what a couple flicks with the knife could do to that face.

"Hey, Louis," the man said.

Louis paused in the open doorway. Did he know this man? Did the bitch show him a photograph? Or was he an acquaintance from one of Denaud's parties, looking for business?

"How are you, Louis?" He climbed the steps. He was smiling and confident, and a warning passed through Louis. This was a man to be cautious with; maybe he was somebody important.

"Do I know you?" Louis said.

"The name is Alex Dartanian."

"Can't place it," Louis said. "Who is Alex Dartanian to me?"

"I'm your judge, jury, and executioner."

Louis grabbed for his gun, but Dartanian twisted his hand before it got inside his jacket. The pain made him step back into the lobby. It all came together then. The move on the gangs in New York and the hit on Storm had to come from this man, not that Cornell punk.

The pressure on his wrist backed him down the hallway. Dartanian threw him against Marie's door and freed his hand. At the same time, he pulled out a Mark I silenced pistol from his shoulder holster. "This is from Stu," he said and squeezed the trigger. The whispered slug caught Louis in the chest. He slid down to the floor with his back against the door, and his eyes looked down into eternity.

Dartanian tucked away the Mark I and closed the main door behind him. As he walked down the steps, he resembled a man going out on the town for a pleasant evening. There was no trace of nerves about him. He looked calm and friendly, like when he first went up those steps. He had the look of a man who had just accomplished a vital piece of business. It was the look of the Protector.

Fourteen

The attack was on. Originally Dartanian wanted to hit Denaud on June 24th, St. John the Baptist Day. The French Canadians celebrated the holiday with massive fireworks displays. He had hoped to use the holiday blasts as cover for his assault. Louis Eglise was dead. The war had begun a day ahead of schedule. There was still a chance the authorities would attribute the explosions midway between Montreal and Quebec to overeager revelers. Dartanian hoped so. He didn't want any interference.

He stepped into the nearest phone booth after leaving Louis among the dead and called Kim Huk's number. A moment later Simara came on the line.

"Our man will be on the alert very shortly," Dartanian said. "Why don't you take in a show?"

"Right," Simara said. He hung up and turned to Kim Huk. "It's showtime."

The Tai Boys stepped out into the hot summer night and followed Simara.

* * *

The lighting at Les Dames was a dim red glow that bathed the customers in a wolfish tint. It changed when the jukebox kicked into gear with a loud rhythm-and-blues song. A blue spotlight cut through the dimness and illuminated a blonde stripper in a cowgirl outfit. The stripper made a quick draw with a silver revolver and blew smoke from the long barrel. Then she began a quick strip.

The crowd enjoyed it, at least those who watched her.

Two tables full of Chinese men on the left of the stage became loud and rowdy, as though they were full tilt drunk. None seemed to pay attention to the stripper.

In the middle of the bar a Japanese man sat alone at a small, circular table with two drinks on it. He wasn't paying attention to the stripper either.

Some customers glanced over at the Chinese trouble makers and appeared to be nervous, but their eyes always fell back to the stripper. They were here to have a good time, and they didn't want any trouble.

The bouncers picked up on the worry and headed over to the tables. One said to Kim Huk, "No trouble tonight, right boys?" He had a set-up look, a smile that flashed before a teeth-smashing punch came.

The young men had seen that smile before. They became quiet, ready for whatever. There was no trace of drunkenness about them.

It spooked the bouncer. "Just keep it down," he said and walked away. He went to the bar and nodded to a man on the other side of the room. Soon there were six large men gathered at the bar, looking at Kim Huk and his company.

Simara raised his hand to summon the hostess passing. It was Cindy Barrington, hustling drinks between performances. Her red hair was long, curly, and wavy. She was showing a lot of skin through the corset-like hostess outfit.

Cindy shrugged. It wasn't her table, but she went to it anyway. Les Dames had trained the women to serve the whims of the customers.

"What would you like?" she said with empty politeness.

Simara crooked his finger and motioned for her to lean over. Cindy rolled her eyes. Men thought they were so cute. She leaned over. "I want to take you home to your father," he said.

Cindy felt a chill. "What did you say?"

He leaned forward, smiling, acting like he was putting the make on her and spoke low. "I want to take you home to your father. Sit down."

Her eyes were mirrors of fear and her face had actually gone pale, making the rouge on her cheeks stand out. Her fingers danced in his palm when he took her hand. She sat next to him and tried to smile convincingly.

"Your name is Cindy Barrington," Simara said. "You were brought into this mess by Jerry Cornell. Your father hired us to get you out of here."

"This is a trick," she said. "No, I can't go. Denaud is testing me."

A gray-haired bouncer with a love for trouble saw the bewildered look on Cindy's face. He saw the Japanese man pulling at her hand while she tried to pull away. He walked over to their table.

"No trick," Simara said. "I'm taking you home." He gestured to Kim Huk.

A table flew in the air and landed on the stage. The stripper screamed and stared at the wild Chinese men. The bouncers descended on Kim Huk. They ran into a well-trained wall of kicks and punches.

Simara got to his feet and pulled Cindy after him.

The gray-haired man stood in his way. "Where the fuck do you think—" he said before the knuckles of Simara's half fist changed his face and mind. He no longer thought about attacking, but about the hammer that came from nowhere and knocked him to the floor.

Cindy tugged against Simara. She didn't understand what was happening. She knew she didn't want to be part of it. She didn't want to risk Denaud's punishment. "We'll never get away," she said.

Simara yanked her off balance and dragged her through the tables. The customers scurried out of the way, abandoning their tables and wondering what the hell was happening. One man threw his drink on the floor and waded into the fight. He was pushed out of the way by one of the bouncers coming at Kim Huk with a wooden ax handle.

Kim Huk turned and blocked the swinging handle with a forearm an instant before it crashed into his head. His right hammerfist swooped in a half circle and crushed the attacker's nose. He went down like a robot with the power cut off.

The Tai Boys moved the fight away from the stage where the army of bouncers had charged. There were more reinforcements running into the lounge of Les Dames, coming from the back rooms and the floors above.

Simara was at the door with Cindy behind him when a man scrambled over a table and jumped with a beer bottle in his hand. Simara dropped Cindy's hand and grabbed the bouncer's wrists with both hands. He smashed his forehead into the man's head. There was a cracking sound, and the man went down like a ragdoll.

The Tai Boys threw chairs, ashtrays, bottles, and anything else they could find to smash the mirrored sections above the bar and the curtained front windows of Les Dames. They succeeded in wrecking the place and smashing exits for their escape, but the tide of Denaud's men swelled and threatened to cut them off.

Sin Simara looked behind him at the outnumbered and unarmed Tai Boys. If they didn't get out soon, the weapons would come into play. Denaud's men were past the shock of a free-for-all and ready to use whatever they had to stop the trashing of Les Dames.

Cindy was stricken with fear. Her panicked eyes darted around the room at the violence and then settled on Simara. The look in her eyes accused him, saying *I told you this would happen.*

Simara could not leave the Tai Boys this way, not when the greater numbers overwhelmed them. The aftermath could be final for the Chinese men. He was about to wade back into the thick of the fighting when a whirling shape jumped through the shattered alcove.

The shape had white hair and a cane, but the cane wasn't for walking. Master Wu charged into the crowd of men surrounding Kim Huk and the Tai Boys. His left fist struck out in a blurring motion. Each time a man fell. He pinwheeled the cane from man to man, knocking down clubs, knives, and guns.

Master Wu moved like a dervish through the crowd. The bouncers wondered how to stop him. Nothing could stop him, and their best course was flight. They were dropping to the floor.

Master Wu fought a path to the door where Simara stood holding the girl. "You tailed us," Simara said.

"Just passing through," Master Wu said. "Take her away. I'll finish here. We can settle up later." He nodded towards Kim Huk, who was fighting a man who stalked him with a wooden chair. "For now I must attend to my student."

Simara dragged Cindy out of Les Dames. She still could not believe it was possible to escape Denaud's wrath.

Denaud's townhouse in Old Montreal was two hundred years old. It was owned by a former member of Parliament who kept it in the family for years. A prime minister had lived there and entertained in a royal manner. Then the house passed down to the intelligentsia and the landed gentry, who provided it with a reputation for cultural "events" that attracted the highbrows in Montreal.

When the taxes and upkeep grew exorbitant, and only the truly wealthy could afford it, Pierre Denaud bought his way into the historical townhouse and quickly stamped his gaudy tastes upon it. The staid French colonial house became a monument to Denaud's career and resembled a Parisian bordello by the time he was through renovating it.

Culture took a dive but the parties continued. Every Thursday night Denaud hosted a soiree for the newly arrived jetset, actresses, politicians, and the usual clique of partygoers who loved to experience the allure of Denaud's gangster charisma.

In the middle of this latest gathering, Denaud received the bad news. First there was the call about Louis Eglise, shot to death outside his mistress' flat. Next, there was the call from Les Dames. It had been attacked. Trashed. One of the girls had been taken.

Pierre Denaud was stunned. He pushed the women away who fawned over him and fought for attention. He thought of Storm and how he was disposed of ultimately, wiped off the face of the earth as though he never existed. He thought of Cornell, but that snake charmer couldn't pull off something like this. Louis was dead and Les Dames wrecked. Somebody was gunning for him. Somebody who knew what they were about.

In the morning he would move to the country estate. He would call the troops and man the fortress until they hunted down the bastard moving against him.

Pierre Denaud was thinking how safe he was in Old Montreal, surrounded by so many civilians and by armed bodyguards when a drunken socialite screamed.

"They've got guns!" she said and backed away from the three-windowed buttress in the corner of the room.

Two dark shapes stepped out of a black Peugeot in front of Denaud's townhouse. An Ingram M10 and a Skorpion M61 chattered simultaneously.

They shot out the windows. As the shattered glass fell inside the townhouse, the party turned into a nightmare. Men and women screamed and lost control of their emotions. They were no longer clever guests to their gracious host. They were a shrieking pack of animals barking for survival.

Every window on the front and side of the townhouse fell. The bullets studded the ceiling with holes. No one was hit, but they had all panicked. Denaud was furious, frightened, and embarassed. Someone had attacked him in his home. He shouted

"Shoot those bastards!" Denaud shouted. "Fight back. Put them away!"

His men were pulling out their automatics when a silver cannister the size of a beer can sailed into the room. A blinding flash and a tremendous shock wave blew across the guests. The roar of the explosion deafened everyone inside.

Denaud's partygoers were stunned and dazed. Mick Porter threw another stun grenade into the smashed window. As the occupants began to recover from the first blast, the second grenade went off. The packed high explosives and magnesium went off like a nova.

Dartanian and Mick got back into the Peugeot and drove off. A minute later twenty people ran out of the townhouse. No one was hurt, but they were all shaken.

Pierre Denaud realized just how vulnerable he was. If those men hadn't panicked and run off, they could have finished him. It was time to hole up in a safe place. He called the country estate to tell the house boss to expect company. "We're getting hit like crazy," Denaud said. "Put some guards by the river and have a man watch the road. Ship every woman and servant out there. I don't want anyone around that will talk to the police if they get dragged into this."

"What's going on?"

"Everything," Denaud said. "We're coming out there to dig in. Some crazy bastard is gunning me. Shoot on sight if you see any strangers."

The Rolls-Royce Silver Cloud dropped Pierre Denaud at his place in the country two hours later. Guy Caisse, now second in command, was with him. Behind the Rolls, a steady parade of cars pulled up to unload their armed occupants. Every available man in his organization had been summoned from Montreal.

There were a few more coming. By the time they all arrived, Denaud would have more than thirty men with him. They were experienced men with blood on their hands. The slaving business made them hard and ruthless and nice to have around at times like this.

They made his place safer. The secluded fortress lay midway between Montreal and Quebec City. It was a wide building, square and colonial, the size of a large hotel or a small palace. Sundecks and towers capped the gray-veined marble structure. The grounds surrounding the estate were cleared 100 yards in every direction.

Marble statues dotted the front of the mansion, elegant and silent reminders of a gentler past. The only concession to modern times were the floodlights that illuminated all sides of the house and a large swimming pool.

In the distance, a ring of forest surrounded the estate, sliced on one side by a gravel drive that led to the main road. There was a small clearing on the other side that led to Denaud's marina where he kept a fleet of yachts. He was not about to be trapped.

Denaud looked on with confidence as Guy filed the troops in. There was nothing to fear. The carloads of men, the pleasant June night, and the stillness of the forest had a soothing effect. It was perfect.

He had two cars down at the main road to keep anyone from turning down the drive that led to his safe house and surrounded it like a moat. He had guards down at his boats.

All was secure. No one could get in without him knowing.

Dartanian crouched in the woods and stared at the huge stone fortress. The place was fit for a prince, but not a Prince of Darkness like Denaud. He was about to be evicted. Alex had three teams scattered throughout the woods, armed from the cache of weapons placed there days ago.

Each ICE man was familiar with the land around Denaud's estate, having spent hour upon hour of surveillance, waiting for the moment to arrive when they could hit it. Now that the general had called all of his troops—as Dartanian had maneuvered him to—ICE was going to strike.

There was a fourth team on the St. Lawrence River, anchored a quarter mile north of Denaud's grounds. The cabin cruiser looked like other luxury crafts on the river. Hidden .50 calibre Browning machineguns were mounted on each side and there were arrow guns for every man on board. The cruiser had been patrolling the wide part of the St. Lawrence River known as Lake Saint Peter for a half hour before Tim Reed anchored them in the small cove.

He looked at his watch. Unless Dartanian notified him the countdown began in five minutes.

Jerry Cornell stared at the blackface camouflage on Lex and Mick. They looked like warriors and they were no strangers to this kind of action. He wondered what he was doing there, sitting in the woods, ready to attack that stronghold in the clearing. Even though they had plenty of weapons, enough for a guerrilla army it seemed, Jerry thought it was suicidal. He crouched there, wearing blackface and looking at the same target.

Lex had told him that the Barrington girl was with Denaud and they would hit them at the same time. Jerry thought back to the moment Lex stepped into his room at The Nelson.

"The three of us are going to attack him?" Jerry had said. "It's crazy."

"It's just another hit."

"Look, I know you're good, I've never seen anybody like you, but we can't do it. Not with three."

"If it makes you feel any better," Lex said, "I rounded up a few guys. I got roots here. I knew who to pick."

"Maybe we should just forget it'" Jerry said.

Lex shook his head. "You can come with me . . . or we can end things right here."

Jerry couldn't picture himself operating alone, maybe with Denaud's men coming after him. He'd decided immediately and climbed aboard the hellbound train.

*   *   *

Four shapes bobbed in the waters of the St. Lawrence. They were the color of night, totally silent as the waves carried them closer to the boats.

Denaud's beachfront had been turned into a small marina. Several pleasure yachts and a high-powered speedboat were moored at a series of docks. A crew of men guarded the docks, but they talked among themselves, laughing and swearing. Their voices carried far, drowning out the sounds not made by waves. The murky shapes in the water split up.

"Enjoy it," one man said. "It's gonna be a picnic." He walked to the edge of the dock and threw a cigarette into the water. Then his steps creaked back down to the middle of the dock.

"Nothing ever happens here," a man on another dock said. "Man, we're out in the middle of nowhere." He laughed at Denaud's paranoia for taking such elaborate precautions.

Two men sat in one of the yachts, smoking and talking low. They were buddies. They shared the views of the other guards. If there was trouble, they would hear it coming in a mile away. "Too bad there's no chicks. The last time I was here, it was like a damn Playboy club."

"Yeah," his partner said. "They probably heard you were coming and took off."

Three more men stood on the grass ten yards from the docks. They were quiet and bored.

"When's our relief coming?" said the man who thought it was going to be a picnic.

He was answered by a grunt.

"What?" he said. He looked over to the next dock, but didn't see the man who'd been standing there a moment ago. He thought the boat was in the way. "What are you doing, playing games?" An iron-fisted hand locked onto his ankle and a dark shape splashed out of the water. "Hey, hey," he said, but he was pulled into the river. A SEAL knife ripped him and sent him to the bottom.

The three men on shore lifted their weapons and pointed in the general direction of the docks. Two shotguns and a rifle swiveled, ready to fire, but they were a split second late. Three black shapes came out of the water, dripping like creatures from the sea. 18-inch steel shafts whooshed through the air and then through flesh and bone. The razor sharp arrows sang their funeral song.

Tim Reed shot a bolt through the neck of the man who looked over the edge of the yacht to see what was going on. He saw the second man aim a pistol at him. Tim rolled backwards off the dock and fell into the water. The other three ICE agents shot their arrows and pincushioned the man before he could fire.

The whole assault took less than a minute and looked like a macabre dance choreographed by a mad god. First the guards realized something was happening. Then they hesitated before going for their weapons. They died without getting off a shot.

The docks were secure. The men in their wet suits took their positions in the boats. Tim Reed ran through the woods towards the cove where the cruiser was anchored.

Larry LaSalle and Red Casey stepped out of the woods at the lower level of the estate. Fifty yards ahead were two cars blocking the entrance road. One man sat on the hood of a Mercedes. Another was inside behind the steering wheel. Every few seconds the inside of the Mercedes glowed from a cigarette.

The second car held two men. Music from a French Canadian radio station drifted out the open windows.

Larry took the Mercedes from the left side. Red

Casey catwalked to the right of the second car and stood slightly behind the front passenger window. Red nodded at Larry and both men fired their Ingram M10s at the same time.

The two men listening to the radio didn't have time to realize what was happening. One minute they had music, the next they had death. 9mm cartridges sprayed the inside of the car from right to left, making light thudding sounds. The Sionics suppressor made the Ingram a touch louder than the car radio.

In the Mercedes, the driver slumped over the steering wheel from a three-round burst of Larry's Ingram. The man on the hood slid to the ground when he heard the silenced slugs. He turned and caught his own three-round burst in the chest.

The sentinels at the road were finished. They'd made the mistake of looking in front, watching the road from left to right. The sentinels never even considered that the enemy had been there ahead of them, waiting for the entire gang to arrive.

Dartanian, Mick Porter, and Jerry Cornell had reached the estate twenty minutes before Denaud. They parked their Peugeot deep in the woods and then joined the rest of the ICE agents already in place.

It was judgment day.

— *Fifteen* —

Dartanian moved to the edge of the woods and slipped a rocket into the launcher tube of the RPG-7. Jerry Cornell looked at the awesome weapon Dartanian had removed from the cache a minute ago.

"Where the hell did you learn how to use this stuff?" he said.

Dartanian pulled the safety cap off the rocket and cocked the hammer. "I travelled a lot when I was a kid," he said. He had three more rockets, two of them speared through loops in khaki straps over his shoulders, and one of them lying on the ground in front of him.

His Skorpion was holstered as was his ASP pistol. A knuckle duster boot knife rested against his calf. Dartanian was a walking arsenal as he stepped out of the trees and knelt on the grass.

The rocket propelled grenade launcher was designed as an anti-tank gun, but in Rhodesia and other Soviet ignited conflicts, the weapon had proved adapt at clearing buildings and shooting hell out of personnel.

He sighted the RPG on the second floor of Denaud's mini-Versailles where most of the activity had been. He waited for the fourth ICE team to go into action.

"Move out when the lights blow," he said.

Jerry nodded. Mick Porter grunted. He was impatiently holding his Ingram with the stock unfolded. An array of clips and grenades hung from his belt, making him look something like a vendor at a night game. He was more than ready to dispense the goods.

The rest of the ICE teams in the woods had Armalite AR-18's and Ingrams scattered among them.

"The line's dead," Guy Caisse said. He glanced over at Pierre Denaud who sat at the head of a long dining table with a glass of wine in his hand.

Until now Denaud had been amused at the situation, holing up in his estate with the best armed slavers money could buy. "What do you mean dead?" Denaud said.

Guy held the phone to his ear again. "Not a sound," he said. He hung up the receiver. "The line's been cut."

A strange popping sound rang around the building, followed by breaking glass. "What the hell is that?" Denaud said. "Check it out, dammit. And what about the men guarding the road? We didn't hear a shot."

The lights on the outside of the mansion went out one by one. A four-man ICE squad each took a side and knocked out the floods, plunging the grounds into darkness.

A half dozen of Denaud's men gathered by the windows of a room on the second floor. They'd turned off the lights in the room and peered outside.

Dartanian pulled back slowly on the trigger of the RPG-7. The booster charge enveloped Dartanian in smoke. Ten yards out, the main rocket motor ignited and kicked the warhead into jet speed. Less than a second passed from the time Dartanian pulled the trigger until the rocket struck home.

The shaped charge burned through the marble wall of the darkened room and sprayed molten rock on Denaud's men. It was like looking down Mount St. Helens when it blew.

Every ICE agent swept towards the estate in the darkness. They ripped the windows on every floor with automatic fire. They stood there and emptied clip after clip. Armalites roared and Ingrams chattered and the Skorpion stung into the trashed palace.

As suddenly as the assault began, the ICE men left the field and retreated back into the woods. Return fire from the estate thudded harmlessly onto the empty grounds.

Dartanian threaded another rocket and blasted it through the front door. Fire swept down the hall in a hurry to scorch everything in sight.

Alex didn't want to destroy the entire building. The ICE surveillance established that Denaud kept an office there with a bank of filing cabinets. Most of the contents would prove to be related to his front businesses, but there would be some links to his real affairs. There always was in cases like this. Denaud thought he was invincible and so he would leave traces of his true connections. It was like a huge web with trapped insects clinging to every strand. Sooner or later the spider would be found, but first they had to get rid of the insects.

Denaud's office was in the rear of the building on the main floor. Dartanian was sure they would find some leads that would take them to the next link.

The strategy was working. Denaud's men began pouring out of the house. Those who had been filled in on the escape route headed towards the marina. Others jumped into their cars. No one wanted to tough it out in a house on fire.

A carload of men screeched away from the attacked palace in a cream-colored Bonneville. They hurtled down the road and would have made it if it wasn't for the roaring Mercedes that bore down on it from the other direction. It was doing at least sixty.

The Bonneville stayed on course for a head on collision until the driver broke and cut the steering wheel sharp. The car thundered off the road and spun around in a 180 degree angle on the grass. By the time the driver regained control, Larry LaSalle and Red Casey were out of the Mercedes raining fire into the Bonneville. They strafed the windshield first and then ran down the sides of the car. The Ingrams whispered the riders to death.

Mick Porter fired a flare gun a half minute after the exodus from the house began. The magnesium blast chased away the night long enough for the ICE men to pour lead into the moving targets. The ICE teams advanced.

The Rolls-Royce Silver Cloud managed to break away. Instead of heading down to the main road it jumped over a small curb and tore up the grass. The headlights flashed over the marble statues that led down to the marina.

Larry LaSalle was caught in the headlights. He turned with an empty Ingram in his hand and saw the man behind the wheel smiling. It was Guy Caisse. Beside him was Pierre Denaud. Three men in the back seat fired sub machineguns out the windows.

Larry took it all in during that year long second. There was little chance. He jumped straight up as the Rolls bore down on him. The front hood hit his legs at fifty miles an hour and levered him down face first. His head thudded into the windshield. The bearded ICE agent flipped onto the roof. His lifeless body hung there for a moment, then dropped to the ground.

Red Casey ran up to the Rolls as it approached and emptied a 20-round clip. It had no effect on the steel armored vehicle. He caught a blast of slugs from a sub machinegun that left teeth marks from the side of his leg to his shoulder. He took three steps back and dropped behind a one-armed statue.

The Rolls swerved to the right and ran a slalom in and out of the statues where the ICE agents had sought cover. Like a trapped rat looking for an avenue of escape, the Rolls bit everything in its way.

The headlights picked out a kneeling form in the distance, the prize at the end of the gauntlet. Guy Caisse stomped on the accelerator and chewed up the grass. He laughed as he neared the crouching man. It was Denaud who realized something was wrong. "Turn!" he shouted. "Turn!"

It was too late.

Dartanian squeezed the trigger of the RPG-7. The warhead of the rocket burned a two-inch circle through the armored front of the Rolls. The blast incinerated every man inside. Molten metal sprayed throughout the shell of the Rolls. The Rolls exploded and sent metal and bone into the sky.

Mick fired another flare. The ICE agents walked among the statues and wasted anything that moved. Tim Reed and the men in wet suits finished off the men who thought they had made it to the safety of the woods. They advanced to the house.

Once inside the burning palace, Mick tossed stun grenades into every room. A trio of ICE agents dove inside and sprayed it with automatic fire.

There were only six men who decided to stay in the house, but they were scattered on every floor and had to be hunted down. One more ICE agent fell from a shotgun blast that took off his face when he dived into a room on the fourth floor. A stunned man stood there with the shotgun, dazed and deafened. It had been a lucky shot.

Mick and Dartanian sawed him in two with a clip apiece. There were no more of Denaud's men left alive. Dartanian hurried down to the back office on the main floor. The house was burning, but there was still a few minutes before it went up completely. He ripped off another clip from the Skorpion and shot open the locked file cabinets. He looked through them quickly, tossing half to the floor, half to the ICE agents waiting beside him.

He picked the files by instinct rather than knowledge, recognizing a few names here and there, but mostly grabbing whatever felt right. It could be a bust, or he could turn up some leads when they fed the information to the ICE computer. There were several folders with pictures of actresses, dancers, and women from ten to forty. He thought the pictures would match up with the missing cases in a dozen police stations across the U.S. and Canada.

When the flames consumed the door of the office, Dartanian packed the selected files into a cabinet and tossed it through the floor to ceiling window. The sudden intake of air fed the flames. A half minute after Dartanian jumped through the smashed glass, there was nothing but a wall of fire in the office.

The building would be gutted, but some of the stone would stand as a memorial to the ICE attack, a message to the slavers. Something was coming after them and it was called justice.

Dartanian handed the file cabinet to Mick and went back to the spot where he'd last seen Jerry. On the way, he heard isolated rounds chattering into the wounded men who littered Denaud's landscape. There could be no survivors. Not one man of Denaud's organization would ever whisper about what hit them.

Jerry was at the edge of the woods. He'd seen some action. There was blood on his boots from the fighting near the statues. He was leaning against the crook of a thick tree when Dartanian approached with his Skorpion hanging by his side.

"Who the hell are all these guys?" Jerry said. He nodded at the black-clad shapes that moved away from the flaming house. His eyes said that he suspected the answer, but he didn't want it to be so.

"They work for me," Dartanian said.

"Yeah, and who are you?" Jerry said. "You're the fucking man, aren't you? You've been playing me along since New York." The military style operation of the precision attack on Denaud had opened his eyes; that and the amount of weaponry and talent at Dartanian's command. "Barrington sent you."

Dartanian looked at the Ingram sitting beside Jerry. "That's right," he said. "I made the hits on the gangs in New York: I hit Storm. Denaud. And now here we are."

"You nailed me," Jerry said. "You pulled it off. So now what? You let me rot in jail forever, that it? Damn, and I trusted you, I followed you, dammit, I followed you! I liked you, don't you see?"

"Yeah," Dartanian said. "So we liked each other."

Jerry looked around. He shook his head at the three men in night gear who had been watching him ever since the fight wound down, making sure he didn't wise up and split. They didn't look away.

"Man, I won't make it in jail," Jerry said.

"You won't make it *to* jail," Dartanian said.

Jerry knew the game instantly and made his play. He snatched the Ingram an inch from the ground.

That's when the Skorpion took him off the board with a three-round burst.

Dartanian shrugged. He had liked some things about Jerry. There had been a camaraderie between them. It was unavoidable, riding out the New York hit together, dealing with Storm, and coming up here to strike at Denaud. Jerry had fought and he probably took out a couple of Denaud's men. For that, Dartanian owed him, but he also owed him for all the women Jerry packaged and sold into ruin.

Jerry had decided on his fate years ago. Dartanian merely provided it.

Sixteen

The July sun streamed through the blinds of the hotel suite. Senator Barrington sat by the window and looked down on the loud hive that was New York City. He had aged considerably during the ordeal but now he was claiming back his old vitality. His voice was loud and his bearing was confident.

His daughter was back and she was in fair shape physically. Mentally, it was another matter. It would take more than time for her to recover from the experience. Cindy's head had been twisted so hard and so often that she joined the ranks of the walking wounded. The pretty redhead was shattered and silent. She needed a psychiatrist, and she needed all the love Senator Barrington could muster.

But she was back. "It's over," he said. "It's over." He sipped at a short whiskey.

"For you it's over," Dartanian said.

Senator Barrington nodded. "You did a hell of a job."

"Damn right," Dartanian said. He stood by the

window with his arms folded across his chest. "I lost two men and a third one has a pound of lead in him. Three of the finest men I know caught it because of me and goddammit, it better not be for nothing!"

"What are you getting at?"

The man in the blue pinstriped suit said, "I hope I'm *getting* to you, Senator." Dartanian lit a Pall Mall and took a short drag. "There's only one of me. There's hundreds of gangs and right now they're probably hitting girls like Cindy. Think how you felt when it happened. And then think about all the daughters out there, millions of them waiting for the wrong man to come around."

Senator Barrington finished the glass of whiskey and set it down on the stand next to the chair. He looked up at the blond man who confronted him with hard blue eyes. "You think I should do something," he said.

"It's your turn to kick some ass," Dartanian said. "I know everything has been all hush-hush so far and your daughter is back and the easiest thing in the world would be to bury this and get on with life . . . but that's how this happened in the first place. Too many people look the other way. Well, you and me, we gotta wake those people up. We gotta go public." Dartanian inhaled again and then put out the cigarette. That's it. End of speech. I think you should educate the public and expose those bastards. What do you think?"

A few days later Alex Dartanian sat in his Cage Street headquarters. With him were Mick Porter and Sin Simara. They were surprised when Dartanian flicked on the television set in the office lounge. He hardly ever watched television, especially the news. It was usually so distorted.

But this was a special occasion.

A minute later they understood. Senator Barrington came onscreen. He had called a press conference to announce the return of his daughter from an international sex slavery ring. The network reporters were skeptical at first, but they showed, along with dozens of other media representatives.

Clips of the conference were given several minutes on the network news program, highlighting the details of Cindy Barrington's captivity. Photos of Cindy were displayed between film of Senator Barrington.

"If not for a gang war that broke out between several factions of the slavers, my daughter might never have escaped. You can see the effects of that war all around you." He discussed the record number of bodies turning up in the streets of New York, all having connections to the slavery trade.

"The chains stretch across the world. Right here in New York. In nearly every major city of the world it exists. The particular chain that took my daughter had a pipeline from here to Montreal and to Nice. From there, who knows where the chain leads."

"Senator," one of the reporters said. "You talked about chairing an investigation into sexual slavery and trafficking in humans, but where will the information come from? Who will dare to talk?"

"I have been contacted by an expert source in the field who has a good deal of experience in investigations and will probably turn up a few leads."

The expert source smiled. "Smart man," he said.

Mick Porter said, "I agree you know what you're doing, but, uh, expert, that's going kind of far."

Simara joined in. "Exactly. Expert is so vague. Just what is an expert?"

"A man who gets things done," Dartanian said.

—————————— *Epilogue* ——————————

Tim Reed dropped the three ICE men off at La Guardia Airport early in the morning, before the August sun had a chance to attack.

Alex Dartanian, Mick Porter, and Sin Simara stepped out of the car and took their lightly-packed luggage with them. There was a festive mood among the men. It was the first time in years that they had actually taken time off from ICE. The three of them were going on vacation.

To Nice.

CELEBRATING 10 YEARS IN PRINT
AND OVER 22 MILLION COPIES SOLD!

☐ 41-756-X Created, The Destroyer #1	$2.25
☐ 41-757-8 Death Check #2	$2.25
☐ 41-811-6 Chinese Puzzle #3	$2.25
☐ 41-758-6 Mafia Fix #4	$2.25
☐ 41-220-7 Dr. Quake #5	$1.95
☐ 41-221-5 Death Therapy #6	$1.95
☐ 41-222-3 Union Bust #7	$1.95
☐ 41-814-0 Summit Chase #8	$2.25
☐ 41-224-X Murder's Shield #9	$1.95
☐ 41-225-8 Terror Squad #10	$1.95
☐ 41-856-6 Kill Or Cure #11	$2.25
☐ 41-227-4 Slave Safari #12	$1.95
☐ 41-228-2 Acid Rock #13	$1.95
☐ 41-229-0 Judgment Day #14	$1.95
☐ 41-768-3 Murder Ward #15	$2.25
☐ 41-231-2 Oil Slick #16	$1.95
☐ 41-232-0 Last War Dance #17	$1.95
☐ 40-894-3 Funny Money #18	$1.75
☐ 40-895-1 Holy Terror #19	$1.75
☐ 41-235-5 Assassins Play-Off #20	$1.95
☐ 41-236-3 Deadly Seeds #21	$1.95
☐ 40-898-6 Brain Drain #22	$1.75
☐ 41-884-1 Child's Play #23	$2.25
☐ 41-239-8 King's Curse #24	$1.95
☐ 40-901-X Sweet Dreams #25	$1.75

☐ 40-902-8 In Enemy Hands #26	$1.75
☐ 41-242-8 Last Temple #27	$1.95
☐ 41-243-6 Ship of Death #28	$1.95
☐ 40-905-2 Final Death #29	$1.75
☐ 40-110-8 Mugger Blood #30	$1.50
☐ 40-907-9 Head Men #31	$1.75
☐ 40-908-7 Killer Chromosomes #32	$1.75
☐ 40-909-5 Voodoo Die #33	$1.75
☐ 41-249-5 Chained Reaction #34	$1.95
☐ 41-250-9 Last Call #35	$1.95
☐ 41-251-7 Power Play #36	$1.95
☐ 41-252-5 Bottom Line #37	$1.95
☐ 41-253-3 Bay City Blast #38	$1.95
☐ 41-254-1 Missing Link #39	$1.95
☐ 41-255-X Dangerous Games #40	$1.95
☐ 41-766-7 Firing Line #41	$2.25
☐ 41-767-5 Timber Line #42	$2.25
☐ 41-909-0 Midnight Man #43	$2.25
☐ 40-718-1 Balance of Power #44	$1.95
☐ 40-719-X Spoils of War #45	$1.95
☐ 40-720-3 Next of Kin #46	$1.95
☐ 41-557-5 Dying Space #47	$2.25
☐ 41-558-3 Profit Motive #48	$2.75
☐ 41-559-1 Skin Deep #49	$2.25

DEATH MERCHANT
by Joseph Rosenberger

More bestselling action/adventure
from Pinnacle, America's #1 series publisher—
Over 14 million copies in print!